Sam had remembered her in his will

Shelly sank into the plush leather chair as the lawyer sorted his papers. Sam had probably felt guilty about all those tips he'd forgotten to leave and left her a few bucks to make up for it. Maybe a hundred dollars, Shelly mused. Boy, what she could do with a hundred dollars. Or even fifty dollars....

"Let me just give you the bottom line," the lawyer said in a slow Texas drawl. "As far as the terms of Sam's will are concerned, he has given you his ranch and made you the majority stockholder of his railroad."

"There must be some mistake." Shelly felt faint with possibility. "What does it all mean?"

The lawyer gave her a reserved smile. "It means that I and everyone else around here work for you. Including Sam's son and expectant heir."

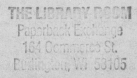

ABOUT THE AUTHOR

Stroke of Midnight is Kathy Clark's twenty-third romance novel. Her own fairy-tale romance with her husband, Bob, helped her come up with this charming spin on the classic *Cinderella* story. She's currently working on several screenplays and, in her spare time, handles guest relations for her favorite baseball team, the Colorado Rockies.

Books by Kathy Clark

HARLEQUIN AMERICAN ROMANCE

Kathy Clark

STROKE OF MIDNIGHT

Harlequin Books

TORONTO • NEW YORK • LONDON
AMSTERDAM • PARIS • SYDNEY • HAMBURG
STOCKHOLM • ATHENS • TOKYO • MILAN
MADRID • WARSAW • BUDAPEST • AUCKLAND

This book is dedicated with all my love to my own Prince Charming—my husband Bob Wernly. He has brought more happiness, laughter and excitement to my life than I ever thought possible. Fairy tales *do* come true!

ISBN 0-373-16571-4

STROKE OF MIDNIGHT

Copyright © 1995 by Kathy Clark.

Printed in U.S.A.

Prologue

The Mexican sun danced across his broad, already-bronzed shoulders as he rolled over on the chaise lounge. The soothing sound of the waves tumbling rhythmically onto the white sand worked its hypnotic magic, washing away any guilt he'd been feeling about this trip. Actually, he had begun to entertain the thought of staying forever, stretched out on the beach with nothing to worry about except keeping his tan even and his glass filled....

"Another margarita, *señor?*"

The man lifted his sunglasses and squinted up at the neatly dressed waiter. "Sure, and send that sexy lady over there another of whatever she's drinking."

The waiter's gaze shifted to a tall, shapely blonde, whose assets were barely contained inside a tiny, black lace, thong bikini. "Ah, *sí, señor.*" The waiter nodded his approval, then headed toward the outdoor bar that offered a limitless supply of cool refreshments for all the guests at the exclusive resort.

As soon as the waiter left, the man dismissed him from his thoughts. After a week of intense business meetings—made even more intense because he was still at the stage where he had to earn the respect of his foreign associates while testing their sincerity and trustworthiness—he was ready to fill his mind with nothing more serious than what he would have for dinner... and with whom he would share it.

He'd been exchanging meaningful looks with the woman several lounge chairs away for the past half hour. She was clearly interested, making sure he noticed when she returned from a swim. Slowly she'd strolled past his chair, crystal drops of water sparkling as they clung possessively to her smooth skin. Sensually she dried off, before taking great care to stroke suntan oil on every inch of her perfect body until she glistened like an alabaster statue in the sunlight. Then, with a suggestive sideways glance in his direction, she reached behind her and unhooked the top of her bikini, catching the bra with her other hand as it fell away, but not before it revealed the full swell of her ample breasts.

In spite of the impressive bait, the man hadn't approached her. Usually it didn't take him so long to act on an attraction. But the midday heat and the lazy south-of-the-border attitude had slowed down his metabolism. But not entirely. He would still be able to put a satisfied smile on her pretty face later tonight, if things should move in that direction.

He relaxed against the canvas chaise and closed his eyes. This was definitely the way to spend the holidays. No hassle, no morning-after mess, no family obligations....

"Uh, *señor*..."

The man looked up, expecting the waiter to have returned with his drink. Instead he saw the hotel manager standing on the sugar-white sand next to the lounge chair.

"A telegram just came for you," the manager said, shifting uncomfortably from foot to foot.

The man couldn't tell whether it was from the hot sand burning through the soles of his shoes or the contents of the envelope in his hand. More to put the manager out of his misery than because he felt any curiosity, the man took the envelope.

"Thanks."

The manager nodded, then hurried away.

The man's movements were leisurely as he lifted the unsealed flap and took out the single yellow sheet of paper that was inside. With a bored yawn, he unfolded it and squinted against the glare as he read.

> I regret to inform you that your father has died. Arrangements have been made and his funeral will be on Friday. Your presence is needed at home as soon as possible.
>
> > Harlan Dickerson,
> > Corporate Attorney, TPRR

Chapter One

"Good night, Frank. Be sure to keep it on the road," Shelly Lowell called to the trucker who was exiting the café. Truckers were the standard fare around the Silver Spur, and Shelly knew all of the regulars.

And they knew her. She could always be counted on to provide good service, honest opinions, when asked, and a friendly smile. But it never went further than that. From the first day she'd dodged a wayward hand, her policy had been not to get personally involved with any of the customers. Sam had been the only one to breach that barrier, and even with him it had never been more than friendship.

The time they'd shared recently, in the wee hours of New Year's Eve had been very special to Shelly. And afterward he'd disappeared into the dark, walking down the deserted street to God knew where, just as he had every Saturday night that he'd shown up on the Spur's doorstep. Several times Shelly had been tempted to follow him, but somehow that would have broken a strange code of honor between them. If he'd wanted her to know more about his private life, he would have told her.

Shelly closed the cash drawer of the register, then turned around and realized that the diner was empty except for the night cook, Clara. But then there always seemed to be a lull between midnight and three each morning.

"Whew!" Clara exclaimed. "Pretty good rush, wasn't it?"

"Yeah, some nights I just don't know where they all come from." Shelly loaded Frank's dishes on a tray and wiped the formica table top. "Do you need any help with the kitchen? I'm cleaned up out here." Shelly started for the back even though Clara would probably say no. As she rounded the corner of the counter, she came face-to-face with the cook, who was holding a cup of coffee.

"Here, go sit down and take a load off. We have a couple of hours before the breakfast crowd." Clara pushed her way past Shelly and placed the coffee in the booth by the door.

"Thanks, Clara. You're wonderful."

"Yeah, well, keep that to yourself," the cook said gruffly. "I've got my reputation to protect."

Shelly rolled her head, stretching her aching neck muscles. She hadn't been sleeping well for the past few nights, and her shifts had been particularly busy. She picked up a used copy of yesterday's newspaper that she had tucked behind the counter for just such a break. "I'll catch the headlines and drink my coffee, then I'll help you get ready for breakfast. Why don't you join me?"

Clara hesitated, her hand on the swinging half door that divided the kitchen from the dining area. "That does sound like a good idea. My feet are killing me. Let me fetch a cup for myself, and I'll be right back."

"In fact, bring the pot." Shelly scooted to the inside of her favorite booth near the door, leaned her back against the wall and propped her feet up on the seat.

"Good idea," agreed Clara as she disappeared into the kitchen. In a moment she was on her way back to the booth with a cup of coffee in one hand and an insulated carafe in the other. She glanced at the newspaper with interest as she sat down across from Shelly. "Is the food section there? I want to clip the coupons."

"Sure, here it is." Shelly pulled the colorful section out and passed it across the table to Clara. They sat, sipping their coffee and enjoying the break from standing on their feet. The diner was almost silent except for the hum of the refrigeration units on the ice machine and the cooler behind the counter and the rustle of the newspaper as they turned the pages. The buzz of the neon sign in the window was punctuated with an intermittent static pop, but neither woman seemed to notice the sound. They were used to it, working as they did almost every night at the diner. Its glowing yellow light proclaimed to all interested passersby that the Spur was open for business twenty-four hours a day. And it often felt to Shelly that she was there for twenty-four hours at a stretch even though her scheduled shift was from ten in the evening to six the next morning.

As usual, Shelly had saved the first section for last, and finally she picked it up and looked at the front page. Her eyes widened as she stared at the large black-and-white photo and the name beneath it. She was frozen for a full minute, not believing her eyes.

"What's the matter, hon?" Clara's voice was concerned as she studied Shelly's face. "Anything wrong?"

"No...no...this can't be!" declared Shelly. "I can't believe it."

"Believe what?"

"It's Sam...my friend Sam." Shelly began to sob as her gaze moved from the photo to the caption below it. "He's dead!"

Her shoulders slumped as the bold, black words on the page continued to stare back at her. She simply couldn't believe that the man she'd danced with less than a week ago was never going to walk through the door again.

Even though he'd denied it, he *had* been ill. She should have insisted that he take a cab or even that he spend the night in the back room. The weather had been unusually cold and damp that night.

Shelly wiped her eyes and stood. Overcome with grief, she excused herself from the table and went to the ladies' room in the corner. The news was hitting her much harder than she would have imagined... almost like when her parents had died or when her husband, Billy...

A fresh wave of tears streaked down her cheeks. She hadn't known Sam long, but he'd become an important part of her life, listening with equal interest to her stories about her daughter, Emily, as he had to her money troubles. He'd always been kind, offering just enough sympathy to help her feel she wasn't alone and sometimes delivering a swift verbal kick to keep her going forward instead of always glancing behind. His words of encouragement when she'd shared her hopes of getting a college degree had kept that dream alive.

And now he was gone forever. No more corny jokes...no more shared tears or dances or cups of coffee. No more Saturday midnights with the man who had become her surrogate father and dear friend.

After a few minutes Shelly felt calmer. She splashed some cold water on her face, took a deep, bracing breath and returned to the still-deserted dining area. But the sadness hung heavily on her heart as she sat down across from Clara. "I just can't believe he's gone."

"Is that the old guy you used to save the apple pie for?"

Shelly nodded, then sighed with disappointment as she read the banner line at the top of the page. "Clara, this is yesterday's paper. I can't even attend his funeral. It was on Friday." Not being able to say goodbye one last time just added to her misery.

"Oh, my Lord...*that's* the man?" Clara exclaimed as she leaned across the table and stared at the newspaper.

"Yes." Shelly glanced at the photo. The same twinkling eyes looked out at her, and the same crisp gray hair peeked out from under a black cowboy hat. But in the picture Sam was several years younger and dressed in the unfamiliar formality of a suit and bolo tie.

"But that's Sam Mitchell," Clara said.

Shelly shrugged. "I never knew his last name, but—"

"I mean, that's *the* Sam Mitchell," Clara persisted.

Shelly didn't understand the significance of that statement, so she returned her attention to the article to see if she could figure out what Clara was getting at.

As she read the lead line, she gasped. She'd been so engrossed with the fact that Sam had passed away that she'd failed to notice the headline.

Sam Mitchell, Owner of the Texas Pacific Railroad Dies in His Sleep.

"I had no idea that your Sam was *that* Sam!" Clara was clearly stunned.

Shelly shrugged. "I thought he was broke and down on his luck."

Clara snorted. "Broke! Sam Mitchell was one of he richest men in this county. Heck, probably in the whole hill country. He could buy and sell this diner in the blink of an eye." She snorted again. "I'll bet he never even left you a tip."

Shelly didn't comment, but that barb hurt. Sam had known, more than anyone, how desperate her finances were. And yet, not only had he never left her even the smallest tip, but many times he hadn't even paid for his coffee and pie.

She rubbed her temples. This was all too much to accept. She'd thought she and Sam were friends. She'd spilled her guts to him in an outpouring of honesty and trust. But now she was discovering a whole new side to his personality—and she didn't like that he hadn't been totally honest with her.

"What else does the article say?" Clara asked, trying unsuccessfully to read the newspaper upside-down.

Shelly had to force her tear-filled eyes to focus on the blurry letters as she read aloud:

"Sam Mitchell, sixty-seven-year-old founder and owner of the Texas Pacific Railroad (TPRR) passed away at his home from an apparent heart attack Monday night. Mr. Mitchell was alone at the time. His only son, Sonny Mitchell, was on vacation somewhere in Mexico and could not be reached, said TPRR attorney Harlan Dickerson.

"Mr. Dickerson held a press conference Tuesday morning at TPRR headquarters as word of Mitchell's death reached the investment community. The TPRR was recently involved in negotiations with the Mexican Government to provide expanded service to the Gulf Coast of Mexico. The direction of the TPRR will be in some doubt, as Mitchell's intent was to expand the railroad domestically rather than pursue the Mexican connection. In an interview with financial backers last month, Mitchell had said, 'The Texas Pacific Railroad was founded on and made profitable by the business of the American rancher. We will not ignore this heritage. They were loyal to us when we were having financial difficulties, and we will not desert them now.'

"This is incredible." Shelly was dumbfounded by the disclosure that he was one of the richest men in Texas. "He never said anything about the Texas Pacific or his son, or anything. In fact, I remember him saying he'd always wished he *had* a son." Shelly found the discrepancy confusing, but in spite of it all, she was still devastated by the news of his death. "I just wish I could have been there yesterday."

Clara reached over and patted Shelly's hand. "Don't be so hard on yourself, dearie. Sam knew you cared for him. He knew what was in your heart."

"He could have told me about himself. It wouldn't have mattered to me. I wouldn't have treated him any differently."

"Take it easy, Shelly. Sam was a fine man, and he must have considered you a good friend, or he wouldn't have dropped by so often."

"I'm going to miss him a lot." Shelly flipped through the rest of the section and was disappointed not to find more about Sam. "Maybe I should contact his son and tell him how sorry I am about his father passing away."

"Let it be. I'm sure there are hundreds of people doing the same thing. You and me are just workin' folk. I doubt his son would care one way or the other what you think."

"I suppose you're right. Sam was a good man. A man of character. But he and his son must not have been close, so I doubt that…what was his name…?" She paused and glanced back at the article. "I doubt that Sonny would know about his father's weekly late-night visits."

Shelly wondered what kind of man Sam's son was. Was he tall and handsome, a younger version of Sam? Was he witty and sweet, honorable and sympathetic like his father? But then how could she speculate on the son, when she obviously hadn't really known the father?

Shelly picked up Clara's scissors and neatly cut out the story. She was especially careful about trimming around the only picture of Sam she would have as a memory. He certainly hadn't looked his age—or acted it.

It occurred to her that he must have been married, although he'd never mentioned that, either. She wondered what had happened to his wife. There was no indication that she'd been with him when he'd died. It hurt to think that Sam had been all alone at that last critical moment of his life.

"Well, you'll have an article to remember your friend by, huh, hon?"

"Yes, I will. I expect there'll be more stories as soon as his son shows up and starts spending all his dad's money. Somehow I suspect Sam and Sonny didn't see eye to eye on the value of a dollar."

"Don't hardly seem worth it to leave it all to your kids, does it?" Clara heaved her bulk out of the booth and headed back to the kitchen with her coffee cup and the empty pot. "Well, I'm sure your Emily appreciates what you've given her a lot more than Sam's son ever did. It seems the less you have, the more you value it in life."

"I just hope Emily doesn't resent that I can't give her more...." Shelly's voice trailed off and she shrugged wistfully. "Ever since she was born, Billy and I had to watch every penny. She's never known any sort of luxury."

"You can't measure love in dollars and cents," Clara said with uncommon insight. "Besides, maybe old Sam left you a couple hundred bucks in his will...you know, to make up for all those nights that you didn't charge him for his meals."

"Don't be silly. Men like Sam don't give money to anyone who didn't earn it," Shelly said, then gave Clara a rueful grin. "I guess it was pretty silly for me to sneak food to a millionaire. Boy, he must have gotten quite a laugh about that at his board meetings."

"I doubt it. Kindness is so rare these days." Clara gave Shelly one of her equally rare smiles. "The old man must have been touched that you liked him for himself, not for his money or his power. You know, someone in his position must have trouble finding people he can trust."

Shelly took her purse from under the counter, carefully placed the article about Sam inside, then returned it to the shelf. "Let's get at the kitchen. The breakfast crowd'll be here in a few hours."

Clara said, "Maybe there'll be more in this morning's paper. It'll be here by two."

They worked hard and fast to get the food and the café ready in time for the morning rush. The Spur served the best sausage-and-gravy country breakfasts along the highway. It was one reason why so many truckers would drive the extra fifteen miles off Interstate 10. Shelly set places at the tables and the counter and refilled all the salt and pepper shakers, as well as the ketchup dispensers. No matter how good the food was, ketchup was always a required additive in a trucker's diet.

Shelly gave the floor a quick damp mopping, even though the drizzling rain outside meant it would be tracked up with muddy boot prints in no time. Twice a week, in the early-morning hours, she added another layer of wax to the permanently yellowed linoleum. No one except the health inspectors ever noticed or appreciated the diner's cleanliness, though it had shown a remarkable improvement since her arrival.

As Shelly paused by the front window, staring absently out at the rain, the newspaper delivery truck pulled to a stop at the vending machine outside. She turned toward the kitchen as she heard Clara walking across the diner floor with a pot of fresh coffee and two cups in her hands.

"Time for one last break. Why not come and sit down for a few minutes?"

"I'll be back in a moment." Shelly propped the mop against the wall and reached into her apron pocket for a quarter as she pushed open the front door. The air was damp and cold, and she wrapped her hands around her arms while the driver cut open a bundle of papers. The rain dripped off the bill of his Rangers' baseball cap as he glanced up after loading the machine. He gave Shelly a damp smile before jumping back into his truck and driving off.

Shelly dropped her quarter into the slot, took out a newspaper and hurried back into the diner. She sat down at the booth as Clara poured the coffee. Before taking a drink, Shelly's eyes widened as she read the front-page article out loud to Clara:

"Future of the TPRR Unclear. Ownership of the Mitchell business and estate is rumored to be clouded. Harlan Dickerson, attorney for the Texas Pacific Railroad (TPRR) eluded reporters today, as questions from the financial community grew in intensity. With nearly $32.4 million in assets, TPRR, controlled by founder, the late Sam Mitchell, has become a matter for the probate courts. Rumors have surfaced, since news of his death became public, that the elder Mitchell did not leave control of the business to his son, Sonny. Sonny Mitchell, age thirty, has been out of the country, but is expected to return to Deer Ridge today. When questioned while leaving his office yesterday, Dickerson said he will be meeting with Sonny Mitchell this weekend. He also said he would have a statement for the press on Monday.''

Shelly sat quietly for a minute. "Can you believe it! Sam's son didn't even have the decency to come home for his father's funeral.'' Shelly shook her head in disgust. "It'd serve him right if Sam gave all his money to charity.''

"I agree. But I'd feel sorry for the people at the railroad. They've gone through a lot of ups and downs the past few years. My husband worked for them but got laid off about two years ago. I'll bet the remaining workers are on pins and needles about the estate being all messed up. Not to mention the little independent ranchers around here. That railroad is all that keeps them competitive with the big guys.''

It was an unusually long speech for Clara, and Shelly could tell that the cook must have deep feelings on the subject. Shelly took a sip of coffee and frowned at the lukewarm liquid. "Want your coffee warmed up?'' she asked as she picked up the pot.

As if she'd used up all her words, Clara nodded.

Shelly carefully filled Clara's cup to the brim and then placed the pot on the table. "Is there anything else in the paper about Sam?''

Clara handed back the section of paper she'd taken from the stack. "There's an editorial on page four.''

Shelly thumbed through to the correct page, then folded the paper open to it. She read aloud:

"Sam Mitchell Will Be Missed. The death of Sam Mitchell marked the end of an era in Texas business. He was the last of the self-made men whose livelihood didn't depend on the oil industry. Forty years ago he took a few hundred dollars and with shrewd investments and hard work parlayed it into a major regional railroad. Through economic hard times, natural disasters and a multitude of labor strifes, Sam never lost sight of the vision he had for the Texas Pacific Railroad. His support of the ranchers and farmers in the remote areas of Texas and the rest of the southwestern United States made Sam and the TPRR the most reliable of friends. The critical question now is: in what direction will the new owner of the TPRR take the railroad?

This reporter believes it's just as well that Sonny Mitchell might not inherit his father's empire. Would he have been able to continue the vision of his father? Certainly his years as a dedicated playboy and accomplished world traveler haven't prepared him for the job. I doubt the younger Mitchell would have been able to devote himself to running a major company. It takes a man who understands that he has obligations not only to the employees and suppliers but to the customers, without which the railroad would fail to exist.

Sam Mitchell did. Too bad he didn't have someone stronger and wiser to whom he could pass on his legacy."

"The more I hear about Sonny Mitchell, the less I like him," Shelly commented in disgust.

The bell over the front door jingled, announcing the first customer of the morning rush. Clara and Shelly left the booth and returned to their work areas. For the next few hours there would be no time to think about anything but getting the food on the tables fast enough.

HE PACED BACK AND FORTH across the attorney's thick cream-colored carpet, a fountain of profanities spewing out of his mouth. Having spent his childhood hanging around railway yards and locomotive roundhouses, he certainly had a vast resource of words from which to choose.

"I can't believe it! What could he have been thinking when he made that will?" He dragged his fingers through his thick, dark brown hair and shook his head in disbelief.

"Now calm down, Sonny—"

"My name is *Jim*," he corrected sharply. "I outgrew that nickname when I was twelve."

"Okay, Jim," the attorney said, his voice soothing. "Don't get so upset. I'm sure your father didn't think you'd be interested in—"

"Hell, the magnitude of what my father didn't know about me would fill the Library of Congress." Jim stopped at one of the tall, brocade-draped windows. His father... He simply couldn't believe the old man was gone. As ornery and shortsighted as Sam had been, he was an institution. And institutions didn't die. Jim turned his back to the room as unexpected moisture filled his eyes.

"You can always contest the will." Even though he was suggesting it, the attorney's tone was doubtful and not encouraging.

"You bet I will." Jim roughly wiped his eyes before stalking back to the chair where he'd dropped his copy of the probated will. "If he thought I'd sit back and let my family's name become a topic of ridicule, then he was badly mistaken. Just because he let some floozy make a fool of him doesn't mean I'm going to accept it calmly. I guess that's what happens when someone starts thinking with their hormones.'' He snorted and rolled his eyes. "I wouldn't have guessed the old guy had it in him."

"Like father, like son," the attorney mumbled under his breath.

Jim gave him a sharp look. "What?"

"Uh...I said your father said she was just a friend."

"Yeah...a friend with her hands in both of his pockets." He flipped through the pages of the will. "What was that gold digger's name again?"

The attorney cleared his throat. "Shelly Lowell. She's a waitress out at the Silver Spur Café."

"And I'll bet she's dancing in the streets about her inheritance."

"Well, I haven't actually contacted her yet. I wanted to talk to you first."

Jim's expression brightened. "If she doesn't know, then I still have some time." He leaned forward, resting his hands flat on the attorney's desk as he asked, "Harlan, for the good of this company and my father's reputation, would you hold off letting this information out for a few more days?"

"I don't know." The attorney frowned and reshuffled the papers on the desk in front of him. "I work for TPRR, and it's my obligation to—"

"I wouldn't ask you to bend the rules under normal circumstances. But this'll have such a radical effect on everyone—" he looked Harlan square in the eyes "—and I mean *everyone* who works for or is serviced by TPRR—that it could cause such a panic the company would never be able to recover." Jim's voice took on an authoritative tone as he straightened and added, "I'll prove she manipulated him and that my father was not of sound mind when he made that will. This company is rightfully mine, and I refuse to let some bleached-blond bimbo destroy it."

Chapter Two

"Good morning, Jim. Did you have a nice weekend?"

"Sure, Virginia. It was just terrific." Jim's voice
dripped with sarcasm, but he knew it would be lost on
the perpetually cheerful secretary.

More as a courtesy than to serve any true function,
his father had given Jim an office as soon as he'd
graduated from Texas A&M University. Virginia,
whose desk was in the center atrium of the corporate
annex, was a part of the package. If only his father
had given him some assignments and responsibilities
to go along with the antique oak desk and efficient
secretary.

"Here are your messages," she said as she followed him into his office. "I'll get you a cup of coffee while you look them over."

She didn't wait for his response, but exited the office and headed down the hall to the small kitchen area
that was shared by all the other executive wanna-bes
who had offices in the annex. It was another of his
father's little jabs to put Jim down with the junior
management trainees. At least there was some logic to
that decision. Jim understood that he should prove

himself before moving up the corporate ladder. But it was back to that old "Catch 22": How could he prove himself if he was never given anything of substance to do?

In a few minutes Virginia returned with a cup of perfectly prepared black coffee which she quietly placed off to his right as he continued to review his messages.

"By the way, Larry Lott from Corporate Security dropped by early this morning. He said he had the information you wanted, but that you wouldn't be happy. I hope you know what that means because I sure don't."

As Jim glanced up, he saw Virginia's puzzled look, but he didn't choose to enlighten her. "You knew my father pretty well, didn't you, Virginia?"

"I knew him for a long time, but I wouldn't exactly say that he and I were close," she answered as she sat nervously on the edge of her chair, apparently waiting for some clue as to the direction of the conversation.

"Did he seem a little...strange the last few months?"

"Strange?"

"You know, different. Maybe even irrational."

Slowly, she shook her head. "No, he seemed fine to me." Her expression lightened. "Actually, yes, he did act a little differently lately."

Jim sat up, his senses alerted. Perhaps this would help his case. "Yes? How?"

"Well, he was..." She paused again, obviously taking great pains to choose the right words. "Happier," she added with a pleased smile. "I can't put my finger on it, but I noticed sometime last summer that a lot of his old spirit had returned. He started circulating around the offices and went to the terminals more. And he was always whistling."

Jim slumped against the plump, leather-upholstered chair. "Whistling, huh?"

"Yes, and he smiled all the time, like he used to. Remember?"

No, he couldn't remember when his father had smiled all the time. Nor could he remember his father whistling.

"Funny thing," Virginia continued, "but he was especially cheerful on Mondays. I noticed because most people are grumpier on the first day of the work week. But Sam would come in rejuvenated, ready to jump right in. I haven't seen him so excited about running the railroad in years."

"Did he mention anything about... dating someone?" Jim watched her face carefully, hoping to read something from her reaction. But all he saw was honest surprise.

"Oh no. He never mentioned anything like that." She shook her gray head emphatically. "I don't think he ever looked at another woman since he met your mom, rest her soul."

"Oh, he looked all right," Jim muttered in a voice too low for her to hear. "Thanks, Virginia. That'll be all for now," he stated more loudly as he picked up his stack of messages, effectively dismissing her. She was certainly not telling him anything he wanted to hear.

She was almost at the door when a solid knock reverberated through the office. Virginia opened the door.

Jim had already recognized his visitor by the powerful pounding, so he wasn't surprised when a tall, sturdily built man entered the room as Virginia left.

"Hey, Sonny, how's it going?" The man crossed the room in long, agile strides and plopped into one of the chairs that faced the desk.

"Not so good."

"Well, you've got a great tan. Shoot, it must be nice to be able to zip off to Mexico for a weekend with a cold margarita and a hot *señorita.*"

Jim gave a derisive snort. "Yeah, like you don't get around."

"Nah, not so much anymore. I've had trouble finding good help, so I've had to spend a lot more time at the store than I'd like." Boomer paused, and a telltale lovesick grin stretched across his face. "And, well . . . Maggie's been keeping me home nights."

"You still dating that cute little cowgirl from Kerrville?"

"Yeah. . . ." Boomer shrugged one broad shoulder almost apologetically. "It's not so bad being tied down to one woman for a change."

"Tied down?" Jim shook his head. "I never thought I'd see the day." It was good to finally be able to let down his guard with someone he could trust. And there was no one in the world he trusted more than Boomer Richards. He and Boomer had been best friends ever since they'd been on the same side of a playground fight in fifth grade. They'd been roommates at college, then even shared an apartment for a while until Boomer's appliance store had started making money. And Boomer was one of the few people who could still get by with calling Jim by the much-hated nickname of Sonny.

Of course, Boomer wasn't *his* real name, either, having been born with the more respectable moniker of Gary Richards. But whether it was the long-standing Texas tradition of saddling children with goofy pet names or the fact that Boomer was always several inches and pounds larger than all the other kids his age, the nickname had stuck. Even today no one called him Gary, and he didn't seem upset by that fact.

Unlike Jim. When he was just a toddler, always following his father on his rounds of the railway yards, someone had commented, "There goes Sam and his little sonny." Unfortunately the name had stuck, and Jim was still struggling to get out from under it. Somehow it represented his lack of individuality, and it was vital that he separate himself from that blindly adoring child who had been but a mere shadow of his father.

"Sorry about your dad," Boomer said. "I know the two of you had your differences, but he meant a lot to this town."

"Well, I'll let you in on a secret. But you have to promise not to tell anyone what I'm about to tell you. Got it?" Jim leaned forward across the massive oak desk and held out his hand.

"Hell, you know I'd take it to my grave." Boomer reached out, slapped Jim's palm, entwined their thumbs and twisted his hand in a backward handshake. It was the same elaborate symbol they'd always used when swearing an oath of loyalty.

Jim remained leaning on the desk as he told his friend confidentially, "My father left the ranch *and* control of the Texas Pacific to some bimbo half his age."

"No!" Boomer was clearly shocked.

"Yes!" Jim stood and paced restlessly across the room to one of the large picture windows that overlooked the railway yard. Absently he watched a huge locomotive leave the warehouse where it had been undergoing some sort of repair, rotate on one of the turntables and then line up for the track that would take it to the terminal where it would be coupled with loaded cars. "I couldn't believe it, either. The old man sure got the last laugh."

"There must be some sort of mistake. Everyone knew that you would take over the railroad someday. And to lose the ranch, too." Boomer shook his head, unable to grasp the magnitude of the news.

The ranch. Although he hadn't lived there for the last half dozen years or so, there was no place on earth Jim would rather call his home than the two thousand acres of rolling pastureland and oak groves where he'd grown up. It had never occurred to him that he wouldn't someday raise his own children there. Being denied that part of his heritage was more painful than being shut out of the company, especially since with the stock he'd been given at his mother's death and on his birthdays, totaling twenty-five percent, he was still one of the major stockholders. But it hurt that his father hadn't trusted him enough to turn over the reins of the family business to him.

"Well, I'm not taking it sitting down." Jim stalked back to his desk and pulled out a yellow legal pad on which he'd been outlining his plan of action. "I've been working day and night with the company security chief and my own attorney since my dad's will was probated on Monday. So far, I've talked ol' Harlan into stalling all he can before he notifies that woman she's the heir to my dad's estate and business." Jim sat back in his chair and took a sip of the coffee Virginia had brought him.

"You hired a detective?"

"I called Larry as soon as I found out about the will's contents. If he isn't able to derail this woman, then it will be up to me to prove my father was not of sound mind and that this woman was nothing but a gold digger, taking advantage of a senile old man."

"Shoot, that's bad...to have people think your father was losing it."

"Yes, but the alternative is worse." Jim could barely contain his anger that everything that should be his could be gone with a few flirtatious winks and the stroke of a pen. He was barely able to hold in his hatred for this woman and to some degree his father. Even in death, Sam Mitchell did not respect his son.

Boomer leaned back in his chair as if to signal his recognition of Jim's outrage. "What information does Larry have about this woman, anyway?"

"I don't know yet. He's supposed to stop by this morning. I'm just hoping he dug up something that'll help me stop this runaway train."

As if on cue the buzzer on his intercom sounded, and Virginia's voice carried through the speaker. "Larry Lott's here to see you."

Boomer stood. "I've gotta run, anyway." He gave Jim a thumbs-up sign. "Good luck."

"Yeah, thanks." Jim smiled and waved. "Send him in," he instructed Virginia through the speaker. Boomer pushed through the doorway, and a short, neatly dressed man stepped inside the room. He was the exact opposite of the stereotypical private eye...a fact that had proven highly effective during his career. Even though he was in charge of security at Texas Pacific, he also kept a healthy private practice going.

"Come on in, Larry," Jim said, mentally crossing his fingers. "Would you like a cup of coffee?"

"Sounds good . . . black is fine," Larry answered as he walked into Jim's office and shook hands firmly.

Jim relayed the information to Virginia through the intercom, then sat back in his chair. "Sit down and tell me everything you know about this woman." Jim still refused to refer to her by her real name.

Virginia returned with a carafe of coffee and a cup and saucer for Larry, then exited, closing the door behind her.

"Well, Larry, give me the dirt on this, this . . ." Jim was so furious, he couldn't find polite words to complete his thought, although he could think of dozens of profane descriptions that he was sure would fit her perfectly.

"Now settle down, Jim. When you hear all I have to tell you, you may have to learn to live with this woman." Larry spoke in his usual calm, low-pitched voice.

"What the hell do you mean by that?"

"I understand your feelings, Jim. But you need to listen to the facts. I can't dig up dirt that doesn't exist, can I?"

Jim was growing more alarmed by the moment. This didn't sound very promising. "Okay, let's hear what you've got so far." He sat back and propped his elbows on the padded arms of the plush executive chair.

"Well, I'll start at the beginning." Larry looked for a moment at his thick legal pad full of notes before he spoke. "Her name is Shelly Lowell. She's twenty-nine years old, born and raised in Atlanta, Georgia. Her parents died in 1984, when she was nineteen years old."

"What did they die of?" inquired Jim.

"A car accident. Seems they were returning home from a routine trip to the shopping mall on Peachtree when they were hit head-on by a drunk driver."

"Any brothers or sisters?"

"No."

"How about an inheritance? Her parents must have left her something."

"They did, but I'm getting ahead of myself. She got pregnant in her senior year in high school and had a daughter, Emily, who's eleven years old now."

"So, she *is* a bimbo!" Jim was inordinately pleased at the news.

"No, just a kid who made a mistake. She married the father, William Lowell. Apparently it was against her parents' wishes, and they had quite an argument. They were still estranged at the time of their death and hadn't even seen the child."

"Where's her husband through all this cavorting with my father?" Jim asked expectantly, still desperately hoping to find a crack in the story.

"After marrying Lowell, she dropped out of high school. Really sad, too, because she'd been an honor student with a 4.0 grade point average up to then. Anyway, she and her husband struggled to make it on their own. He went on to college while she worked at an automotive assembly plant to pay the bills. Then when her parents died, she used the insurance money to help put Billy through law school. Along with a few government loans, he finally graduated and was offered a job with one of the best law firms in Atlanta."

Larry stopped a minute and flipped back and forth through his legal pad, collecting his thoughts.

"Is there anything else?"

"Just wanted to get this all straight. From all I could find out, she sacrificed everything so Billy could get his degree and establish his career. He baby-sat while she went to night school and got her GED. Things were just looking up for them when Billy found out he had leukemia. He struggled for nine months before dying. Of course they had no insurance, and the debts mounted."

Jim saw that Larry was really moved by Shelly's story, which only increased his own aggravation.

"So how's she been supporting herself since then?"

"Well, she tried to make a go of it in Atlanta, but finally packed up the kid and headed west to Phoenix where Billy's parents lived. They'd moved there after Billy graduated from high school. Unfortunately her car broke down here. They wired her eight hundred dollars to get the car fixed, but it was beyond repair, so she took the money and settled with Emily in an apartment over the Silver Spur Café. Seems Pete, the owner, felt sorry for her and sort of took her in."

"So she was stranded here? How long ago?"

"The middle of July."

"And since then? Who's she dating? What kind of mother is she? Who all has she slept with?" Jim was intentionally crude as he grew more frustrated.

"As far as anyone who knows her will say, she hasn't dated anyone. And I have found no indication that she sleeps around. Apparently she was extremely loyal to her husband, and he was her first and only boyfriend." Larry shook his head. "I just don't think she's that type."

"That type!" Jim repeated angrily. "It sounds like she charmed you just like she did my old man."

"I'm just telling you what I've discovered." Larry didn't look away from Jim's piercing blue eyes. "And I did a *very* thorough investigation."

"But there's nothing here that will help my case."

"No, Jim. Nothing," Larry agreed. "Let me go on. It tells you a lot about Shelly."

Jim shrugged and leaned back in his chair as Larry continued.

"She took the night waitress job because it paid more than working the day shift. And it also gave her time to be with Emily after school. She gets by solely from the tips and five bucks an hour Pete pays her. He charges her only one hundred and fifty a month for the one-bedroom apartment, but there are lots of other expenses—"

Jim interrupted. "So, she's been trying to save enough money to get a car and move to Phoenix?"

"At first that was her plan. But everyone, including Shelly herself, told me that she really likes it here and is in no hurry to leave. Emily's doing well in her new school and is making friends. Shelly's tips are growing and she opened a savings account a few days ago."

"How much does she have in it?" Jim asked eagerly.

Larry gave him a wry smile. "A whopping $105.17, to date."

"Well, where is all the money my dad gave her?" Jim knew his father must have been generous. His father had a soft heart and always gave to a variety of charities. Jim was certain she must have benefited greatly from his father's wealth.

"I found no evidence that she received any money from your father, Jim. None whatsoever. In fact, the cook was positive that Shelly wasn't even aware of who your father really was."

"Like hell she wasn't!"

"No, really. Apparently she thought he was a homeless bum."

Jim snorted and shook his head in disbelief. "What a crock! You're making her sound like Mother Theresa."

"She seems like a genuinely nice person who's just had a run of bad luck. She has no possessions to speak of, no other accounts around town and hasn't sent any money to anyone except for small payments to her creditors since she's been here." Larry glanced over the last few pages of his notes and checked off several items he had covered.

"When and how did she and my father get involved? How many people knew about it?" Jim asked, tiring of the dead ends he'd been encountering ever since Larry had sat down in his office.

"That's a little harder to get a handle on, I'm afraid. I posed as a local newspaper reporter doing a series on people who work all night. I got a lot of news about the people who frequent the diner and work along the highways in these parts—"

Jim interrupted again. "I suppose you're going to tell me my father was a busboy on the night shift at the Spur. Come on, Larry, I need something that'll expose her and prove my father wasn't himself when he left all this to her." He swung his arm in a wide arc, indicating not only the office, but the entire railroad company and its acres of warehouses and miles of tracks.

Larry gave Jim a shrewd look. "How much did you know about your father's habits? It might help if you had a little inside information." But it was obvious that Larry already knew the answer to his question. Everyone around Deer Ridge did. It was common knowledge that Sam had pretty much washed his hands of his playboy son, banishing him to the outer offices and not allowing him to sit in on the meetings of the board of directors.

"I didn't know his friends or even all of his business associates. And we never went out together socially. What are you getting at, anyway?"

"It seems that Sam had been visiting the diner every Saturday night around midnight. He met Shelly there just after she started working at the Spur. I wasn't able to find anyone in town who knew of them being together except for Clara, the night cook at the Spur, and even she never actually saw him. She'd heard Shelly talk about her visitor, but she hadn't suspected it was your father. Did you know about these midnight excursions?"

"It's news to me. What do you make of it?"

"Well, Sam seemed to be really taken by her kindness toward him and would sit and talk with her for hours. As far as I could discover, they never went anywhere. Just sat there in the diner and talked. I honestly don't think she knew who he was." Larry's grin was genuinely pleased. "Boy, is she going to be surprised when she finds out about her inheritance! She—"

Jim burst to his feet and cut off Larry in midsentence. "She will *never* see a dime of my father's money nor set foot in this company. I'm going to head this railroad from here on. We're going to move forward with my plans to link with Mexico. I'll drag this company into the twenty-first century if it takes the rest of my life."

Larry stared at Jim for a moment, then began gathering his notes into a neat stack. "It looks like I've done all I can. You're on your own from here on."

Jim exhaled a heavy sigh as he realized he was not handling the situation very well. If he was going to be in charge, he'd better learn how to control his emotions, especially in front of his employees. In a much calmer voice he said, "Listen, Larry, I appreciate what you've done. I'll call if I need anything else." He reached out and shook the detective's hand.

Larry turned toward the door, but Jim stopped him. "Would you mind leaving your notes? I'd like to look over them again. Maybe you're right about this... woman. She certainly sounds like a saint."

Larry hesitated, then took the notes out of his portfolio and slowly, as if with great reluctance, extended them toward Jim.

"Thanks." Jim smiled and walked the detective to the door. After returning to his desk, he heaved another sigh and sat down. Resisting a natural urge to toss the notes into the wastebasket, he took an empty file folder out of his drawer and tucked the notes inside. Who knew when the information might come in handy. Although, if it didn't reveal anything more dastardly than that she'd gotten pregnant before marriage, he wouldn't have a snowball's chance in hell of winning the judge's sympathy over her sad life story. It all sounded like one of those B movies that made women reach for their hankies and bored men out of their skulls.

Jim sat quietly in his chair and stared out the window that ran the length of his office. As if taunting him, he had a clear view of his father's corner office on the fifth floor of the main wing of the building. Jim had been relegated to the slums of the annex while the nerve center of the company was two floors up. It was on that top floor where the executive directors and the corporate attorney had their offices next to the boardroom...the floor where policies were made and careers broken. Here Jim sat, so close yet so far from the power source of Texas Pacific.

Oh, sure, he knew he could take advantage of the situation and move into his father's old office until the court case was settled. But his pride held him back. He knew he could do great things for the company. But he wouldn't sit in his father's chair until he'd proven himself.

"Jim, can I get you anything?" asked Virginia from the doorway between their offices.

"No. Uh...wait. Yes, there *is* something. Get Hal York on the phone." Virginia nodded and returned to her desk. While he waited, Jim tapped his fingers on the polished-oak surface. Maybe the internal auditor could help find a crack in the fairy-tale story of Ms. Shelly Lowell.

"Mr. York is on the line," Virginia said over the intercom.

Jim punched the flashing button at the bottom of his phone and said, "Hello, Hal. Jim Mitchell. Wonder if you could do me a favor?"

"Sure, Jim, anything."

"I'd like you to check and see if there were any unusual payments made from either my father's personal account or any of the corporate accounts to a Shelly Lowell in the last couple of months."

"Jim, I know what you're trying to do. I've been over all this with Dickerson and your attorney. We can't find anything." There was a nervous pause, then Hal said, "Give it up. Unless you can make a case within the next few days, Shelly Lowell will have to be contacted and informed of her windfall."

So that was how the wind was going to blow, Jim thought with disgust. Whatever happened to loyalty? He could understand why they didn't feel any allegiance to him personally, but surely they could see the advantages of continuity. How could they hope a silly, uneducated, inexperienced—in the boardroom, not the bedroom—woman could take over the controls of such a complex company and not run it into bankruptcy?

"You know we all thought the world of Sam." Hal's voice ended the lengthy silence. "Believe me, if there was anything I could do, I would."

"Yeah, right. Thanks, Hal. Bye." Jim hung up the phone and laced his fingers behind his neck. Slowly he leaned back in the chair and stretched as if to wake himself from a long, deep sleep...complete with nightmares. Once again he considered his options, few as they were. He still couldn't believe this was happening to him. His father couldn't have hated him that much. Surely there must have been some misunderstanding, something that would have corrected itself had he not died when he had. Or maybe it was all some sort of cruel joke in an attempt to shake Jim up, preparing him for his responsibilities. In fact, maybe he would wake up and discover his father wasn't really dead at all, sort of a new twist on "A Christmas Carol."

Jim leaned over and opened the bottom drawer of his desk. Reaching way in the back, his fingers encountered the cold brass edges of a picture frame. Glancing around as if afraid someone might see him, Jim withdrew the object and gazed down at it, emotions churning inside him.

There in the photo a tall, handsome man was holding up a small boy so the child could pull the horn in the cab of a locomotive. The man was smiling proudly, but it wasn't his expression that captured Jim's attention. It was the open adoration on the boy's face as he looked down at his father.

What had happened in the years since that five-year-old boy had worshiped the man whose arms held him so securely? When had his father stopped loving him? When had the family ties been broken?

Jim blinked away another annoying rush of tears and replaced the photo at the back of his drawer. Well, he would prove the old man wrong. He knew he had a battle ahead, not only to regain possession of his company and his home, but to make the Texas Pacific the most powerful, profitable railroad in the United States.

The first thing he had to do was to break his father's will. And it appeared the best way to do that would be to discredit the woman who stood to gain everything.

Jim picked up the file folder and dropped it into his briefcase. His first mistake had been to trust the wrong people. Since he had the most to lose, he was obviously the person who would do the best job getting the truth. And the only way he could do that was to go to the source.

Yes, he would get "up close and personal" with Ms. Sugar-and-Spice-and-Everything-Nice Shelly Lowell. He would find out what really happened and how she'd taken advantage of his father. He'd prove she was just another bimbo with tight buns and loose morals.

After all, she probably didn't know him from Adam. He doubted his father had spoken about him and certainly would never have shown her a picture. If she was as shallow as he thought, she'd be easy to fool.

Jim smiled, confident of his own abilities to win her over. Then, after he'd gotten what he needed . . . and maybe more if she was as sexy as he was sure she'd be . . . he'd crush her under his heel.

Chapter Three

As Jim turned the sleek black Corvette off the county road onto Highway 83, he gripped the leather steering wheel and accelerated until the wide tires sprayed out a shower of gravel. The road was nearly empty as he drove the half-dozen miles from his apartment complex on Horseshoe Lake to the Silver Spur. His mind practiced again and again his opening lines for when he walked into the Spur and met Shelly for the first time.

He shook his head as he thought about the shabby job Larry had done. Jim had been expecting dirt, but he'd gotten sugar instead. Clearly, domestic cases were not Larry's strong suit.

He rounded a turn and saw the faint glow of a flashing yellow light on a tall sign in the distance. As he drew closer, the image cleared until it became a giant spur, its rowel appearing to spin as the spikes of light rotated.

Jim slowed his Corvette and pulled onto the vast parking area that dwarfed the stone and stucco building. The small diner looked like an island surrounded by a sea of asphalt. But since its major clientele needed the extra space to position their eighteen wheelers, it was a necessity to maintain business. Several beer signs glowed from the windows and a round neon sign alternately flashed Fine Food and Hot Coffee around the words Open 24 Hrs.

Although he hadn't been inside since his senior year in high school, he recalled seeing a framed, faded newspaper article that had hung on the wall over the cash register, announcing the diner's grand opening on May 1, 1947, which was about seventeen years before he was even born. Oddly enough, the place had always looked the same, embracing a sort of casual, rundown charm that made people immediately feel at home . . . or, in the case of the more cosmopolitan customer, fearful of food poisoning.

He parked his car at the side of the building, not wanting whoever was inside to draw any premature conclusions. Tonight he was playing a role. Tonight he had a mission. Tonight he was going to take the first concrete step toward regaining his inheritance. This was his best chance to gain the upper hand in the battle for his father's estate, and he was ready to pull out all the stops. If there was a weak link in Shelly's story, he'd find it.

He still couldn't imagine why on earth his father had chosen to spend his Saturday nights at a place like this. There was obviously a difference between how a self-made man liked to spend his leisure time and the way a man born into wealth and influence liked to spend his.

Before pushing open the heavy glass door, Jim peered between the slats of the metal blinds and was relieved to verify that there were no customers inside. Deer Ridge was a small town, and almost everyone would know him on sight. He couldn't afford to be recognized while talking with Shelly.

However, the only person he could see through the window was a twenty-something brunette standing behind the counter reading the newspaper. The flashing yellow neon light splashed color on his tanned skin as he reached forward and eased the door open, hoping to gain a few more seconds of quiet observation before he had to go into action.

But he was betrayed by the bell. At the tinkling sound, the waitress glanced up at him as he momentarily paused in the open doorway. She smiled and nodded as if to say hello...just hello. There was nothing flirtatious or even overly interested in her expression, except as a waitress to a customer. Instead she looked tired and thin, as if she hadn't had a whole night's sleep or a good meal in a long time.

Her hair wasn't frizzy blond like he'd imagined, but long and silky looking, pulled back into a thick French braid. A silly-looking pink lace cap was pinned on top of her head, but wispy bangs and long tendrils had escaped to curl around her face. He'd expected thickly mascaraed eyes and ruby red lips. Instead her soft, if slightly too-pale skin showed few signs of makeup, and her lips were full and a warm shade of rose that looked too natural to be lipstick. She was average in height, but his experienced eyes knew there was an attractive figure beneath the unfitted and somewhat oversize uniform. It surprised him that she was pretty in a gentle, subtle way, not at all flashy and trashy as he'd assumed. Of course, this woman may not even be the person he was hoping to meet. Shelly might have taken the night off.

Then again, this could be her. He actually had no idea what she looked like. And besides, looks could be deceiving. Her innocence could be how she attracted her victims.

With just a brief glance from several feet away, her eyes seemed to sparkle when she looked up at him. He walked deliberately to the lunch counter and selected a padded stool in front of where she was standing. As he began to lower his six-foot-one frame onto the seat, his gaze rested momentarily on the generous swell of her bosom before settling on the name on her badge . . . Shelly.

"Hi, mister. What can I get for you?" Shelly asked as she folded the newspaper and set it aside on the counter.

"Well, I don't know." Jim frowned at the surprisingly nervous lilt of his voice and consciously lowered it as he added, "I'm not real hungry. Maybe just a cup of coffee and a piece of pie for now."

Shelly looked at the pie display. "We've only got apple left."

"Fine. That's my favorite." As she turned away to fill the order, Jim glanced at the folded paper and noticed she'd been reading the latest article about how the TPRR would deal with his father's passing. He steeled his features so they wouldn't show the negative reaction he always had when people who had little or no knowledge of the inner workings of the company speculated on its future. Instead, he forced his gaze to shift casually, and he grinned in Shelly's direction.

She returned the smile almost immediately. "You're lucky there's any pie left. It's a popular late-night choice." She placed the thick china plate in front of him, then reached down and arranged a napkin, fork and spoon properly next to the pie. She picked up the pot and poured a cup of coffee. "Here you go, sir. Anything else?"

Jim realized he'd been staring at her, and he gave himself a mental shake. *Be cool,* he reprimanded himself. *You have a lot at stake here. This is no time for your hormones to kick in.* Playing the game was one thing, but he couldn't afford to feel any sort of attraction to this woman...even just physical. "No," he told her, forcing his eyes to focus on the late-night talk show on the small television at the other end of the bar. "I'm okay for now. It feels good to finally get here. Been drivin' for the last four hours. The stripes were beginning to hypnotize me, so I thought I'd better take a break."

Shelly took a tray of ketchup bottles out of the refrigerator along with a large jug of ketchup. As she talked, she unscrewed the tops of the smaller containers and filled them from the jug. "Where're you heading?"

"Jim. Call me Jim." He studied her face for a reaction, but when her expression didn't change, he breathed an inward sigh of relief and continued with the story he'd been rehearsing. "Well, actually I'm heading here, I think. Tomorrow I thought I'd look for a place to stay and maybe try to get a job over at the railroad. Friend of mine says they're hiring again."

Jim wondered if he was forcing too much information on her, so he stopped and took a deep breath as if to be relaxing after a long day of driving. A couple of sips of coffee and a bite or two of pie allowed several moments to pass without further comment.

Finally Shelly finished her task, tightened the last lid and returned everything to the refrigerator. She picked up a towel and wiped her hands as she returned to stand across the counter from him. "Yes, I heard they're hiring again, too. It's supposed to be a good place to work when things are prosperous. It's terrible when companies fall into a bad economic cycle...hiring and laying off, hiring and laying off. Hope you have better luck."

"Me, too." He took another bite and said with studied casualness, "You live around here...Shelly, isn't it?" He pointedly looked at her badge.

"I have an apartment upstairs."

He glanced upward. "Looks like it must be pretty small."

"It's tight. But it's just my daughter and me, and we make do." She shrugged, but he caught the hint of wistfulness in her voice as she added, "We didn't bring much with us when we moved, so it's not all that crowded." She filled a glass with water from the refrigerator's spigot and dropped a few ice cubes in it. "How about you? Any idea where you're going to look for a place to live?"

"Well, I haven't planned that far ahead. Something close by probably. Any ideas?" Jim realized he was relaxing as the conversation flowed smoothly between them. This was going better than he'd imagined. Well, sort of... He hadn't exactly found out anything yet, but he was getting to know Shelly Lowell a little better.

"I can ask Pete," she answered. "He owns this diner and rents me my place. If anyone would know what's available in this town, Pete would."

He gave her one of his most charming grins, hoping to sneak a little information from her about her plans for her future. "Any chance of you moving out soon?" His tone had just the right level of lightheartedness. Shoot, he should have been an actor!

Shelly returned his banter. "You'll have to leave a pretty hefty tip tonight if I have any hope of moving soon." Her gaze swept his intentionally casual and inexpensive cowboy shirt and faded jeans. "Somehow I have a feeling there's no hurry for me to start packing."

Jim caught himself smiling. A genuine smile, not one he was using for effect. And it annoyed him. Her openness and her lack of pretense caught him off guard. And the gleam of intelligence in her eyes disarmed him even more. It wasn't a shrewd, calculating cleverness, but a quickness, a warm wit that he found—or rather *could* find—very appealing. Under different circumstances.

And those eyes. . . . What a strange and fascinating color they were. Not quite green, but not quite brown, and surrounded by the longest, thickest lashes he'd ever—

Good Lord. He was completely losing it. Speculating on her eye color wasn't accomplishing anything. This woman was trickier than he'd imagined. She was subtly sneaky, making him be attracted to her against his will. Well, he'd just show her he was too smart to be sucked into her little trap. It was time he took back control of the conversation.

"Mind if I ask what happened to your husband?" He returned his full attention to his pie and asked the question with what he believed was a perfect balance of nonchalance and concern. Not too much that she'd think he was prying, but just enough so she'd think he was a caring, sensitive man.

He glanced up in time to see the piercing look she gave him. It almost made him squirm on his stool. It was as if she was peering into his very soul, measuring his sincerity and deciding whether or not to trust him. For a few seconds he held his breath, part of him hoping she'd fall for his act...and part of him hoping that he was right about her intelligence and that she wouldn't be fooled. He honestly didn't know whether or not he was disappointed as she answered.

"He died five years ago of leukemia." Shelly grew quiet and looked away from Jim, but not before he saw the shimmer of tears fill her eyes.

Even though he already knew of her husband's death, Jim was moved by the depth of emotion in her voice. "I'm sorry to hear that. I just lost my—" He caught himself before he said the word that would have brought this farce to an end. It was apparent he was losing perspective of his mission at the Spur. Shocked at his loss of focus, he steeled his resolve. "I guess that made quite a change in your financial picture."

"It sure did. And still does. I have school loans to repay, and we didn't have any insurance. No one thinks they'll die young. It's just not...right." Shelly glanced in his direction and managed a smile that was obviously forced. "More coffee, Jim?"

He nodded and pushed his cup closer to her side of the counter. "Enough of that kind of talk. How old is your daughter?"

"She's a very mature eleven-year-old." Shelly filled his cup, then stood, still absently holding the pot as her expression softened. "She's held up well to all the changes in her short life. I'm really proud of her."

As he sat mapping out his next series of questions, Shelly interrupted his train of thought.

"Okay, I've told you about me. What about you? Why come to Deer Ridge? Texas is a big state."

"Me?" Jim was startled. He hadn't counted on having to trade life stories to get what he wanted from her. He'd already told her everything he'd rehearsed, but apparently that wasn't going to be enough. He was even more surprised by the ease at which she was able to put him on the defensive. He stalled the response as long as he felt possible without shutting off the open communications they had developed.

"Well, it's not all that interesting," he said ad-libbing, desperately wishing he'd paid more attention in his drama classes. But they'd just been snap courses to fill in the spaces around the requirements for his business management degree. "I was born in Alabama in 1964, but we moved to Dallas when I was a kid. My father worked as a switchman for the Texas Pacific until he died. He was fifty-eight. My mom had never worked outside the home before, but she had to start cleaning other people's houses to make ends meet." He shrugged and shook his head. "Nothing special about my childhood." Jim looked expectantly at Shelly in hopes that her curiosity was satisfied.

"Married?" Shelly asked.

"Nope. Haven't done that yet," Jim responded, pleased with her interest. He waited, his mind whirling with possible answers to her questions about his relationships, then was disappointed when she didn't pursue the subject.

Jim pushed his half-empty coffee cup across the counter toward Shelly. "I could use another cup. This is really hitting the spot tonight."

"Sure...glad you like it. I usually don't make the coffee. Clara does."

"Clara?"

"She's the cook who works with me every night." Shelly freshened his coffee, then went to work making another pot. "She went home early with the flu or something. It'll get real exciting around here when the breakfast crowd starts coming in at four-thirty."

"You have to handle it all by yourself?"

"No, I called Pete and he's going to have the day cook come in a couple of hours early." She placed a filter in the basket and measured coffee granules into it. "I'm not a bad cook, but I could never handle the rush. People get crazy when you overcook their eggs."

Jim caught himself smiling again and neutralized his expression. "Sounds like you never get a day, or should I say a night off." Jim hoped his comment would give him an opening to ask Shelly out. Not that he really wanted to...but he needed to dig a little deeper into her life and habits and motives.

"Oh, Pete's not a complete slave driver. I get Sunday and Monday nights off."

Ah-ha. She was setting the trap...or so she thought. But he was on to her. Now the conversation was going just as he'd planned. He moved in for the kill. Ducking his head in what he knew was a "golly gee" movement women found irresistible, he said, "I was wondering, Shelly...uh, I know I'm new around here and you don't know me...yet..." He lifted his gaze and stared directly into her eyes. "But I've really enjoyed this time here tonight. Would you be interested in going out with me next weekend? Maybe we could take in a movie and have dinner before...?'' Jim felt himself looking expectantly at Shelly again.

She turned away, picked up a tray and busied herself walking around the small diner and collecting the salt and pepper shakers. "I appreciate the offer," she answered from across the room as she looked over her shoulder. "I've really enjoyed talking with you, too. Trouble is, I have so little time with Emily that I make it a point to do something special with her on my nights off. And just yesterday she found out she has the role of the fairy godmother in *Cinderella* at her school. I've got to get her costume made, help her with her lines and a million other chores."

It took a few seconds to sink in. She'd turned him down! He couldn't believe it. This had to be another part of her plan. So... he'd have to adapt his own to keep her from winning this round. "Well, I've never been rejected because of a fairy godmother. That's original."

Shelly placed the loaded tray on the counter, and the glass containers rattled against each other. She paused long enough to toss him a defensive look. "It's the truth. If you're still around in a few weeks, you can drop by the elementary school and see the play for yourself."

"I'm sorry, Shelly. I was really hopin' you'd consider going out with me. I guess I'm—"

"It isn't you...exactly. You seem like a nice enough guy. It's just that my spare time is valuable to me."

"Sorry. I just thought..." Jim gave her one of his best pitiful looks and shrugged. "Never mind." He got up from the stool that had been his base for the past hour and reached in and pulled out his money clip. "How much do I owe you?"

She reached into the pocket of her apron and pulled out a pad of guest checks. But before she filled it out, she paused. "Look, don't take this wrong. I've enjoyed talking to you. But it's a personal policy of mine not to date the customers. Besides, I don't even know your last name."

He translated her last statement as a sign of weakening, so he moved to take advantage of it. "Would you say yes if I told you my last name?"

She gave him a half smile, but didn't hesitate as she answered, "No. But I'd know you better the next time you came in, wouldn't I?"

Her deliberately confusing response didn't go unnoticed. But he'd be damned if he knew how to interpret it. For a long moment he tried to think of a way to work himself out of the corner she had painted him into. Finally he chose to keep it light. "You're right. I guess I came on too strong." He gave her his "guaranteed-to-succeed" crooked grin. "As they say in the movies, I shall return!"

She clicked her ballpoint and scribbled on the top check. "Cup of coffee and a piece of pie. That'll be $2.34."

Jim peeled off a five-dollar bill and placed it on the counter in front of her. "Keep the change." He focused on her face, trying to will her to lift her gaze so he could look into her eyes. But she kept her gaze lowered, her eyes shielded by the dark fringe of her lashes. His voice softened. "I really did have a nice time, Shelly."

"So did I," she murmured, still not looking up.

Jim turned and walked toward the door. He kept his steps slow, in hopes that Shelly would change her mind or say something to encourage him further. Behind him, he could hear the rattling of his pie plate, cup and saucer. As he placed his hand on the door handle, he glanced back at her. "Connors."

Shelly looked up . . . and smiled. It was not a flirtatious smile or even an encouraging smile. It was more of a gentle, friendly gesture. "Well, Mr. Connors. Do stop in again real soon. And good luck with that job."

"Job? Oh, right." For a moment he'd been dazzled by the sweet beauty of her face. "Uh . . . thanks." Then, with more force than absolutely necessary, his hand tightened on the handle and he jerked the door open.

Round one was over—and the winner was . . . ?

Damned if he knew.

He stalked to his car, opened the door and slid slowly into the low, rich leather seat. Through the perpetually dusty diner windows, he could see Shelly disappear into the kitchen with the dish tub. He felt his lips curve into a smile, then again remembered that he'd failed to accomplish his mission. He slammed his fist against the steering wheel, pushed the key into the ignition and started the car. He was glad to be leaving.

"Boy, Bernice, am I glad you're finally here." Shelly slid a spatula under a sizzling fried egg and flipped it over. The broken yolk leaked a yellow trail out to surround the circle of white. "Darn . . . that's the third one I've ruined . . . ."

Bernice put her head through the circular strap at the top of her apron and looped the strings into a quick bow behind her thick waist. "Here, let me take over before you cut all the profit." Without waiting, she took the spatula out of Shelly's hand and pushed the younger woman aside. "It must have taken you all night long to make such a mess of my kitchen."

Shelly collapsed on a tall kitchen stool and took the first break she'd had for two hours. "It was pretty slow around here until around three. Actually, there was only one customer...." Brilliant blue eyes, sometimes piercing, sometimes twinkling, pushed into her thoughts as they had so often since that cowboy'd left the diner just after midnight.

Hundreds of men walked in and out of the Spur every week. Why, then, had this one made such an impression? Sure, he had the tall, dark, ruggedly handsome looks of a man more accustomed to making his living modeling designer shirts or tailored slacks than someone who was trying to find manual labor. But good-looking men in tight jeans were a dime a dozen in Texas. And it certainly hadn't been his personality, because, although he'd seemed outgoing enough, she'd sensed a wariness that had tempered his actions and words.

And yet, there'd been something about him that had pulled her gaze to him time and time again, when she should have been focused on her work. The rich baritone of his voice had caressed her ears, and his warm, husky chuckle had made her feel strangely young and lighthearted.

"A man."

Shelly blinked as Bernice's voice abruptly brought her back to the present.

"I said," Bernice repeated with a sly, knowing smile, "from that silly look on your face, that one customer must have been a man."

Shelly felt an unexpected blush creep along her cheeks and decided it would be wiser to change the subject rather than pursue it. "Uh . . . I managed to keep up with the crowd until around four. But everyone must have decided to hit the road at the same time today. We haven't had an empty table or bar stool since then."

"Well, I'm here now, dearie." Bernice glanced around the kitchen as she simultaneously flipped three strips of bacon and took some toast out of the toaster. "Run along and get some sleep. You've done enough damage here for one day."

Shelly looked at the dusting of flour, where she'd sort of overshot the bowl when she'd mixed the biscuit dough, and at the specks of grease that had spattered onto the countertop. There was a slice of toast on the floor that she'd dropped when it had burned her fingers and some charred remains of overcooked eggs on the grill.

"I'm sorry. Things were just so hectic." She slid off the stool and picked up a roll of paper towels. "I'll clean it up."

The bell over the door tinkled at the same instant that someone clanged the service bell by the register.

"Get out of here," Bernice ordered, softening the harshness of her words with a fond chuckle. "Annie's going to be a little late today, so could you make sure Linda has everything under control out there before you leave? We wouldn't want some of those customers to decide to take their chances at O'Donald's down the road."

All ten stools were still occupied, but a couple of tables were now empty, waiting to be cleared as their customers stood at the register with checks and cash in hand. Shelly took care of them while Linda cleared the tables. They were almost instantly filled as new customers filed in. Shelly circled the room, refilling half-empty coffee cups, while Linda delivered glasses of water and menus.

"All the orders up on the clips?" Bernice asked, barely looking up from the Spanish omelet she was folding as Shelly walked into the kitchen with the empty coffeepot.

"All caught up, Bernice. If we fall behind now it's your fault." Shelly gave her co-worker a teasing smile.

Bernice returned it with complete confidence. "Just leave the cooking to the pro."

Shelly returned to the dining room with a fresh pot of coffee and began filling the new customers' cups. She barely looked up when she heard the front door open again, but after placing the pot on the warmer, she turned to the newcomer.

Dressed in a dark business suit and red "power" tie, he stood in the doorway, holding a briefcase in front of him and looking very out of place in the roomful of truckers and other casually dressed locals. He glanced around the room until his gaze settled on Shelly, then walked over to the cash register at the end of the counter.

Shelly decided the man must need change for the newspaper or pay phone or wanted a cup of coffee to go. She stopped at the register and gave him a welcoming smile. "May I help you?"

"Are you Shelly Lowell?"

Shelly was surprised by the question. No one ever came looking for her. In fact, very few people around here even knew her last name. After a moment's hesitation, she answered with a hint of wariness. "Yes. I'm Shelly Lowell."

"Do you have a place we can talk?" The man looked around the crowded room as if what he had to say was a top government secret.

"Is anything wrong?"

"Not really. I just need to pass along some information to you that I don't think you want anyone else to know... at least, not yet."

The bell over the door tinkled again as more customers arrived. Although they headed toward the restroom, she knew they'd be expecting their menus and coffee as soon as they returned. "Will it take long? I'm very busy."

"No ma'am. But we really need a little privacy."

"We can go into Pete's office, I guess. Come with me." Shelly leaned into the kitchen as they passed the door. "Could you watch the register, Bernice?" she asked. "I'll be in Pete's office for a few minutes."

Bernice's expression was curious, but Shelly didn't stop to explain. Besides, she had no idea herself what the man wanted. She led the way to a door marked Private next to the men's room. Apprehensively she turned the knob and stood aside, allowing the man the opportunity to enter first.

Pete's office was very small and cluttered with stacks of papers, piles of sports magazines and boxes serving as file cabinets. The walls were covered with pictures and newspaper clippings with one photograph, a signed black-and-white glossy of Roger Staubach, taking the place of honor over Peter's desk. The desk, stained with numerous cigarette burns along the front right edge, took up one whole wall.

The man stopped as soon as he stepped inside, unsuccessfully hiding a grimace as he looked around. It was the first change of expression Shelly had noted, but his face resumed its dour look as he turned and faced her.

"This is as private as we've got," Shelly told him, nervously closing the door. But she didn't move away, choosing instead to lean against the wooden barrier. She didn't stop to question if she was unconsciously allowing herself a quick exit or a way to call for help if she needed it. Her gaze again traveled over the man's conservative outfit. Not that anyone dressed like an undertaker was likely to attack her. "Now, what's this about?"

"My name is Charles Spurrier, and I'm a representative of the Texas Pacific Railroad." He gingerly placed his briefcase on top of a tipsy stack of papers on Pete's desk and snapped open the latches. "You knew Sam Mitchell?"

"Why yes. He was such a nice man."

"Well, Ms. Lowell, Mr. Mitchell must have thought highly of you, too." Charles lifted the lid of his briefcase and removed an envelope. "We've been trying to locate you since we probated his will last week. He named you in it."

Shelly interrupted. "Sam remembered me in his will? How sweet of him." He'd probably felt guilty about all those tips he'd forgotten to leave and had left her a few bucks to make up for it. Maybe a hundred dollars, she mused. Boy, what she could do with a hundred dollars. Emily needed a new pair of tennis shoes and some material for her fairy godmother costume. Or even fifty dollars....

"I'm not authorized to give you any details at this point," the man continued. "In the envelope is a letter confirming this meeting and the direct phone number of Harlan Dickerson. Harlan is the chief counsel for the company. He'd like you to call him as soon as possible and make an appointment to see him. At that time he'll fill you in on all the specifics." He held out the manila envelope toward her. "Call anytime after 9:00 a.m. But try and do it today. Harlan is attempting to get this wrapped up." Charles nodded a farewell, then walked out the door.

Shelly followed him to the door, then stood looking down the empty hallway, somewhat dumbfounded by the news. Imagine...Sam had remembered her in his will. But before she could drift into further speculation, a shout from the kitchen interrupted her thoughts.

"We need help out here. They're stacking up out there like jets over Dallas International!"

Shelly pushed her hopes of a windfall out of her head and closed the door of Pete's office behind her. She helped Linda until the other waitress, Annie, arrived at seven-thirty. Shelly finished checking out the people who were waiting at the register before she took off her apron, told everyone goodbye and practically crawled up the outside flight of stairs to the apartment over the Spur.

Once inside, she knocked on the bathroom door. Over the noise of running water in the sink she shouted, "Are you about ready to go, Emily?"

Her daughter shut off the water and opened the door. "Hi, Mama. Do I look okay?"

Shelly's gaze slid approvingly over the pink turtle-neck sweater and black skirt that Emily had chosen to wear. The little girl's long, dark brown hair was neatly combed, but she was struggling to fasten a barrette in the back to hold the sides away from her face. Shelly took the barrette from Emily and slid it into place, then snapped it shut. "You look great, honey. I can't remember...do you have rehearsal after school again today, or is it tomorrow?" On the heels of the news she'd just received from her mystery visitor, Shelly's tired mind simply couldn't recall her daughter's schedule.

"It's tomorrow, Mama. Tricia's mom's going to pick me up after school so I won't have to ride the bus. Is that okay?"

"Sure, honey. I've got an errand to run, but I should be back by the time you get home."

"Okay. I'll see you later." Emily put on her coat and picked up her books from the living room coffee table. "I got up late and didn't have time to wash my dishes. I put them in the sink, and I promise I'll do them as soon as I get home."

"No problem." Shelly walked to the front door and opened it. "Better get out of here or you'll miss your bus. 'Bye, honey," she said as she gave her daughter a hug and a kiss on the cheek.

"'Bye." Emily hurried out of the apartment and down the stairs, then skipped across the parking lot to the school bus stop at the edge near the county road.

Shelly watched for a moment, filled with motherly pride. She truly couldn't ask for a more wonderful daughter than Emily. The child was so self-reliant and undemanding. With the wisdom of a person well be-yond her eleven years, she never asked for things she

knew her mother couldn't afford. In fact, she tried
very hard not to be a burden and to help make Shelly's off-hours easier. It was one of Shelly's greatest
regrets that she couldn't give Emily more. If ever a
child deserved a special treat, it was her daughter.
Perhaps if there were a couple of dollars left from
Sam's endowment, she would take Emily to a movie.

Shelly waited until her daughter climbed aboard the
big, bright yellow school bus, then she shut the apartment door and walked into the kitchenette. She spent
several minutes washing the few dishes and generally
cleaning up, trying very hard not to fantasize about the
contents of Sam's will. After all, it couldn't be very
much. If it had been, some mention would surely have
been made in the paper. She'd collected all the newspaper articles and tucked them away in an envelope,
but she remembered their contents.

In the background Emily's clock radio still blared
from the bedroom. "It's eight o'clock and time for a
weather update from Jerry Glanzer. Take it away
Jerry...." Shelly went into the room and pushed the
Off button. She yawned and rubbed her eyes. It was
still too early to call that Harlan person. Maybe she'd
lie down for a little nap and call him when she woke
up. Then she could catch a few more hours sleep before or after the appointment, depending on when he
was available. Shelly pulled back the comforter and
kicked off her shoes. Without even bothering to undress, she curled up on the still-warm sheets of the
double bed she and Emily shared. Except for her days
off, she and her daughter slept in shifts.

"Thank you, Sam," she whispered, her eyelids
drifting closed. "You didn't forget me...."

Chapter Four

Shelly rolled over and peered through squinted eyes at the clock radio. The digital numbers shifted to display twenty after three. *Twenty after three!* She sat up so abruptly that the comforter slid off the bed into a pile on the hardwood floor. Sam...the will...Mr. Dickerson...

She hadn't meant to oversleep. In fact, she hadn't gotten eight consecutive hours of sleep in days. Of course she would choose today, of all days, to go for a new record!

The envelope was on the table next to her purse. She took out the letter and glanced over it, but there wasn't anything in it that Mr. Spurrier hadn't already told her. Now all she had to do was call Mr. Dickerson and hope she could get an appointment. It was probably too late for him to have an opening in his schedule today.

"Mrs. Lowell?" his secretary repeated after Shelly identified herself over the phone. "Mr. Dickerson was hoping you'd call. Of course he'll see you this afternoon. How soon can you get here?"

"Uh...thirty minutes," Shelly answered, caught off guard by the secretary's enthusiasm. They sure were anxious to pass on the fifty or so dollars Sam had left her.

"Good. I'll tell Mr. Dickerson. We're located in the main building, room 506."

Shelly said goodbye, then hung up. As she hurriedly stripped off her wrinkled waitress uniform, she couldn't believe how accommodating they'd been. They must just want to get this whole issue wrapped up, and she was probably the last, since her bequest was the smallest.

For several minutes she couldn't really spare, she stood in front of the tiny closet she and Emily shared. Actually, her selection wasn't all that great, but she wanted to dress properly. She wouldn't want Sam to be ashamed of her. Finally choosing a pleated black skirt, white blouse and burgundy blazer, she took a quick shower, dressed, then brushed her hair and put on a light shade of lipstick. She stepped into a pair of midheel black pumps on her way to the door. Just as she opened it, Emily bounced up the stairs.

"Hi, Mama. Are you just leaving?"

"Yes, I'm running a little late. I'd ask you to ride along, but this is sort of a business meeting."

"That's okay. I've got lots of math tonight. Old Mrs. Grayson must think we don't have anything else to do but homework."

Shelly grabbed her coat from the couch where she'd tossed it earlier. "I'll hurry back. There's some hamburger meat defrosted in the refrigerator. We'll have dinner as soon as I get home."

"Are we going to have spaghetti?" Emily asked with delight.

"Sure." Was there ever a kid who didn't love spaghetti? "Lock the door," she called as she stepped outside and headed down the stairs.

A few minutes later Shelly carefully eased Pete's ten-year-old car into the parking space in the visitor's area of the Texas Pacific parking lot. She was ten minutes late and didn't pause to glance into the rearview mirror to recheck her hair and makeup. It didn't matter, anyway. She would be in and out of there in less time than it had taken her to drive to the company.

Pushing aside her feelings of anxiety, she walked into the building. The receptionist directed her to the fifth floor, and Shelly waited nervously for the elevator. Even though she had often visited her father at his accounting office, the formal atmosphere of the business world always made her uncomfortable.

She found room 506, opened the door to Mr. Dickerson's suite and walked in. The carpet was very plush, completely muffling her footsteps as she crossed the room. Around her, dark walnut paneling lined the lower half of the walls, while the upper half was papered in a hunter green fox-and-hound pattern.

On the far side of the large outer office a trim, attractive woman in her mid-forties was efficiently typing on a keyboard at her desk. Shelly guessed this was the woman she had spoken with on the phone earlier. Before Shelly could speak, the woman looked up and smiled.

"You must be Mrs. Lowell," she said as she stood and walked toward Shelly. "I'm Mary Sands, Mr. Dickerson's personal secretary. Can I get you a cup of coffee or a soft drink?"

"I'm fine, thank you."

"Please have a seat and I'll let Mr. Dickerson know you've arrived." Mary walked to the tall double doors that apparently led to the attorney's private office, opened one and closed it behind her as she went into his room. In what seemed like a matter of seconds, both doors swung wide and a tall, rugged-looking, gray-haired man filled the doorway.

In a slow Texas drawl the man spoke to Shelly as he crossed toward her. "Afternoon, Ms. Lowell. I'm Harlan Dickerson. Welcome to the Texas Pacific. Did Mary take care of you?"

"Yes, thank you, Mr. Dickerson." She extended her hand toward his. "It's nice to meet you." Harlan's warm, firm handshake put Shelly at ease.

"Please. My friends call me Harlan. And you and I are going to get to know each other real well, I think. Why don't you come into my office, and I'll explain why I wanted to talk with you today."

Shelly preceded him into his office and sat on the overstuffed chair he indicated. Harlan's inner office was very similar to the decor of the outer office. Square in the center of the very large room was a massive oak desk with three other chairs like hers facing it in a semicircle. Before seating herself, she had noticed that the entire wall behind her was one contiguous bookcase. She recognized the large sections of volumes with matching bindings as law books.

The view of the railway yard spread beneath the large fifth-floor windows that wrapped around the northwest corner of the building. Shelly knew that only the highest-ranking people in a company got the corner office, which further impressed her about this meeting with Mr. Dickerson.

"Thank you for finding time in your busy schedule today, Ms. Lowell."

Shelly had to swallow back a nervous giggle. *Her busy schedule.* "Please . . . call me Shelly," she said, hoping to feel more relaxed on a first-name basis. The day was overcast, and she was able to see Harlan's face more clearly as he sat down in the chair behind the desk.

"I'm sorry I was so secretive about what this is all about. I needed to minimize the number of people who knew about the contents of Sam's will . . . prematurely. I won't bore you with the reading or the legal language unless you insist upon it. Let me just give you the bottom line." Harlan pushed back from the desk and opened the center drawer. He pulled out a large legal file and opened it on the desk in front of him. He slid his chair closer, picked up his half-moon reading glasses and placed them carefully on his nose.

Shelly edged closer to the front of the chair as if to hear better. She grasped the ends of the arms of the chair to steady herself. The money would mean so much to Emily.

"Apparently, Sam thought highly of you. No one, including myself, knew anything about this will until it was opened. He'd changed it just weeks before his death, using an attorney across town." Harlan looked down at the documents, then back at her. "Anyway, according to this, you were his best friend and he believed in you."

Shelly sat amazed. "I didn't even know Sam's last name until I saw his picture in the newspaper. I had no idea he even had any money. He seemed almost penniless by the way he dressed." Shelly really didn't understand anything about her relationship with Sam. "Do you have any idea why he wouldn't tell me who he was?"

"I suspect that in his later years Sam felt that everyone was trying to get something from him. Even his boy, Sonny, was putting pressure on Sam to do things he didn't agree with. Anyway, regardless of his motives, here are the highlights of Sam's last will and testament." Harlan paused and removed his glasses, placing them neatly on top of the closed file before beginning. Apparently he was completely familiar with the will's contents and didn't need to refer to it as he continued.

"Basically, as far as Texas Pacific is concerned, he has given you thirty-five percent of the railroad, which makes you the majority stockholder. Forty percent of the remaining shares are spread out among some investors and old friends, and the other twenty-five percent is owned by his son. You now hold the title of chairman and chief executive officer of the Texas Pacific Railroad unless the shareholders decide otherwise."

"There must be some mistake." Surely she couldn't have just heard Harlan say that Sam had left her his company.

But Harlan was giving her a reserved smile. "It's not a mistake. Sam's will was very clear."

"No," Shelly protested. "I can't believe he meant *me*. Surely there's another Shelly Lowell…there must be some mistake."

Harlan shook his head. "There's no mistake."

She swallowed a dozen more protests, settling instead on an almost frantically asked "What does it all mean?"

"It means that I, and everyone else around here, work for you." Harlan didn't relax a muscle as he added, "Congratulations."

She wasn't sure if he'd spoken with sincerity or sarcasm. Either way, she was in a total state of shock. The magnitude of it all overwhelmed her. "I'm not prepared to handle this. I don't know anything about running a railroad...."

Harlan's attitude softened slightly. "You seem like an intelligent, personable young woman. Leading the company will be the easy part. Each department has a manager. They'll fill you in and help you get the feel of things. Of course, I'll be available to give you an overall picture of operations and help you in any way I can. But first you'll have to deal with Sonny. As you can expect, he was shocked to hear about the terms of this will. He thought all along that Sam would leave the TPRR to him." Harlan lifted his hands in a gesture of dismissal, as if he wanted to make it clear he had not taken sides with Sonny.

"I've assumed the liberty of talking to all the executives about the change in ownership," he went on to say. "They've agreed to stay on for a minimum of ninety days until you decide who you want to keep on staff."

"I'm in no position to make any major changes." Shelly leaned back in her chair, her mind whirling with all of her new responsibilities, still not believing this was happening to her. "The newspapers said that the TPRR is operating at a profit, and I wouldn't want to jeopardize that." She sighed. "I'm really sorry about his son. I imagine this was a double blow on top of his father's death."

"Not only is he upset about Sam leaving you control of the TPRR, but he's very unhappy about Sam leaving you his ranch."

Shelly sat up straighter. "His ranch? Sam left me a ranch, too?"

"Lock, stock and barrel. Two thousand of the prettiest acres in the area. Along with a four-bedroom, twenty-five-hundred-square-foot house, three barns and about five hundred head of livestock, you've got quite a spread."

"Where will Sonny live if I have the ranch?"

"Oh, don't worry about that. Sonny hasn't lived at home in about ten years. He and Sam never really got along, so Sonny moved out as soon as he graduated from college."

"What was the problem between them?"

"Among other things, Sam wanted to keep the railroad focused on the bread-and-butter customers that made the TPRR what it is today—the ranchers and farmers in Texas and the rest of the Southwest. Sonny wanted to expand the railroad south into Mexico. With the recent passing of the North American Free Trade Act, Sonny's plans became more feasible... and potentially profitable. But Sam wouldn't consider giving up old customers for an unknown, especially when a foreign government would be involved." Harlan pushed his chair back from the desk and stood up. "So, are you ready to start work?"

"No. Not really. I don't know where to begin." Shelly was overwhelmed by it all. A company to run, a two-thousand acre ranch, a house of her own, a new life for her and Emily. They wouldn't have to share the same bedroom or worry about paying their electric bill. Emily could get braces and that new pair of shoes, and Shelly could even afford to buy a camera to take pictures of the school play.

Her thoughts screeched to a stop. Would she have time to even see Emily with all the added responsibilities?

"Let me give you some more of the details," Harlan added, no longer relying on his memory, but referring to a legal pad on which he'd written a list of notes. "Sam provided for you to receive a $50,000 per month salary as chairman and CEO, and of course his checking and savings accounts will be turned over to you. You'll have his old office down the hall, and his Ford Bronco. The ranch has a staff of three full-time people—a cook and maid, a ranch hand to take care of the livestock and a personal assistant to keep things organized and handle odd jobs. If you have time, we'll take a ride out to the ranch this evening. I'll give you the keys to the ranch house then." Harlan walked around the edge of the desk and sat down against the front edge. In a soft voice he assured her, "I'm here to help you succeed. A lot of us are. We realize you're in an unusual situation, and we'll do all we can do to help. Just ask."

"Thanks, Harlan. I truly am overwhelmed." Her temples were throbbing with the beginning of a headache—probably the first of many she'd be having during the next few weeks as she learned her new role. And for her daughter's sake, she would learn her role well. But, at the moment, all she wanted was to get away and think things through. And she had to fix dinner for Emily before they went out to the ranch, which meant she would need to arrange for a replacement at work. "Harlan, I need to call Pete, the owner of the Spur, and let him know I won't be coming in tonight."

"Tonight? Better tell him you won't be coming back at all."

That thought floored her. For some reason it hadn't even occurred to her that that part of her life, too, would change drastically. "But I'll have to arrange to move my things. They're in an apartment upstairs I'm renting from Pete—"

"I'll take care of everything. I'll arrange for the corporate moving company to pack your things and take them to the ranch, if that's all right with you."

"But Emily and I don't have very much—"

"That's okay. You've got enough on your mind without worrying about little things like that. This way, you won't have to lift a finger." Harlan stood up and extended his hand to Shelly. "Welcome aboard. I'll arrange a small lunch in the executive dining room for tomorrow, so you can meet all the key people. Would that be convenient for you?"

"I . . . yes, of course it would."

"You can use my phone to call Pete if you'd like. It'll take me just a few minutes to make the arrangements for this evening and tomorrow." Harlan walked to the door, opened it and left.

Shelly walked around Harlan's desk and sank slowly into his chair, savoring the feeling of the rich leather supporting her body, feeling like Cinderella slipping her foot into the glass slipper.

HARLAN'S MERCEDES SEDAN turned off the main road onto the asphalt driveway that led into Sam's ranch. Over the entrance was an arched sign with the words D-Rail painted in black on the sparkling white wood.

"Sam named the ranch after his wife Dee," Harlan explained. "He used to joke that she derailed his obsession with the railroad when they fell in love."

A large, wrought iron gate stretched across the entrance, and a small speaker was mounted to a post on the left side of the driveway. As the car came to a stop in front of the gate, Harlan lowered his power window, waiting until the glass slid silently down before reaching out and pressing the button on the speaker box.

"May I help you?" said a statically blurred male voice.

"Yes, Joe. It's Harlan. I've brought Ms. Lowell and her daughter to see the ranch." Harlan raised his window without waiting for a reply. As the window neared the top, the iron gate began to open. "You'll like Joe, Shelly. He's been Sam's personal assistant for fifteen years. He was the one who drove Sam to your diner every Saturday night. I suppose he knew more about what Sam was doing than anyone."

"Mama, is this our new home?" Emily asked as she peered out the back windows at the dusk-shadowed countryside.

Shelly had told Emily about the inheritance, and the little girl had taken the news more calmly than her mother. Shelly was still having trouble believing all this wasn't some sort of fairy tale. She half expected to wake up at any minute and realize she'd overslept and was late for work. Of course, she hadn't gone into great detail with Emily. There would be time enough to explain it all, when things were more settled ... more definite.

The car began the slow drive toward the ranch, which lay a quarter mile up a narrow road that wound around huge, ancient live oaks. In the near darkness, their twisted arms took on strange, spooky shapes and formed a lacy umbrella over the drive.

The sprawling single-story ranch house finally came into view, looming large against the last orange splash of the sun sinking into the foothills. The building was made of fieldstone that was native to the area. The steep, shingled roof sloped down to cover a wide wooden porch that stretched all the way around the house. There was white wicker furniture scattered in comfortable groupings, and on the right side a hanging swing shifted gently in the breeze as if Sam's ghost was sitting there, watching his property transfer to its new owner.

Shelly shivered at the thought. She didn't mind so much that Sam's ghost might be hanging around the place. After all, according to Harlan, Sam had built it stone by stone and loved it third-best, next to his family and his railroad. What bothered her was that she might somehow fail Sam. She had no business experience and had never even owned a house before. What if she didn't live up to his expectations? What if she made foolish decisions and ruined the railroad?

"Sam," she whispered, resting her forehead against the cool glass of the passenger's window, "I'll do my best. But please be patient."

"Did you say something?" Harlan asked.

Shelly lifted her head and turned to him. "How long ago did Sam's wife die?"

"I believe it was about fourteen years ago. Sonny was sixteen or seventeen, and it's hard to say who took it worse, him or Sam. They both worshiped her."

"What did she die of?"

"Dee battled breast cancer for years. They caught it too late to do anything for her." Harlan shook his head sadly at the memory. "She tried her best to get those two hardheaded men to make their peace before she died."

"So this hostility between father and son has been going on for quite a while."

"For as long as I've known them. But I've heard they were inseparable when Sonny was younger." Harlan gave her a wry smile. "If you ask me, their real problem was that they were too much alike. Once Sonny got old enough to have an opinion and voice it, he and Sam started bumping heads. Each was convinced that his way to do things was the only right way." Harlan parked the car in front of the house and turned off the key. "Well, are you two ladies ready to take the grand tour of your new home?"

"Are we really going to get to live here?" Emily asked. Her eyes were wide with wonder as she looked at the huge house.

"If things work out, we may move in here tomorrow," Shelly confirmed, still hesitant to be too definite just in case the situation changed. The little girl had had enough disappointments in her short life.

They all opened their doors, and Harlan hurried around to join Shelly and Emily on their side of the car. Standing at the foot of the steps, waiting expectantly, were two men and a woman.

"These folks have been with Sam for years. If I were you, I'd trust them to help you with the transition. They're still upset about Sam's death, and they're hoping you'll keep things intact, at least for a while."

"Just like with the Texas Pacific, I'm not planning on making any major changes," Shelly assured him.

"Sam was a good judge of people. Anyone who won his loyalty has mine."

"I'll introduce you to them. Just remember that you're the owner now. They know that and they want to take as good of care of you and Emily as they did of Sam."

"Okay." She took a deep, steadying breath. "Let's go."

"Folks," said Harlan, smiling, "this is the lady I was telling you about...Shelly Lowell and her daughter Emily."

The three people smiled and stood quietly as they awaited their turn to meet the new owner of the ranch.

Harlan stood slightly behind Shelly and Emily as he made the introductions. "Shelly and Emily, this is Joe Santiago, Sam's personal assistant. He handles all the day-to-day tasks that keep things running smoothly around here. Joe and his wife Janie live on the property in a cabin on the other side of that big hill."

"Pleasure to meet you, Ms. Lowell. If there's anything I can do, please don't hesitate to call on me," Joe said, while gripping her hand firmly with his callused fingers.

"Nice to meet you, too, Joe. But you have to call me Shelly."

"And this is Rosa," Harlan continued, "Sam's...I mean *your* cook here at the ranch. She used to work for Sam's favorite restaurant and he talked her into working full-time for the D-Rail."

"Good afternoon, Señora. Maybe we could get together when you have a chance and work out a menu with your favorite meals," Rosa said, her words heavily accented, but easily understandable. "Señor Sam liked roast beef and mashed potatoes."

"I'm sure whatever you've been cooking for Sam will be fine for us, won't it Emily?" Shelly asked, looking at her daughter.

"Yes, it'll be fine. But if I have a choice I like spaghetti—"

"We'll get to that later, dear," Shelly said.

Moving to the last person in the line, Harlan said, "And this is Baker. He runs the ranch and takes care of all the livestock. He also lives here, in an apartment over the stables."

"Hello, Baker." Shelly gave him a friendly smile. "Is that a first or last name?"

"First name, ma'am. My father had a weird sense of humor, I guess."

"Well, I'm glad you're here. I haven't spent much time around animals, so I'll be relying on you completely in that department."

Emily's expression brightened. "Animals? There are animals here? Oh, Mama, can we get a horse after we move in?"

"Well, maybe..."

"Actually, you have ten horses already," Baker commented in a slow, shy drawl. "Maybe I can take Emily to see them tomorrow."

"Yes, yes, please, can he?" Emily was holding Shelly's hand in a death grip and practically jumping up and down in her excitement.

"Sure, that'd be great," Shelly agreed, then added, "After school, of course."

"Of course," Baker said, giving her an understanding nod.

"Okay, you can all get back to work or—" Harlan glanced at his watch "—I guess it's about time for you all to go home. I'm going to show Shelly and Emily around the house, then we'll lock up. They'll be moving in tomorrow, so there'll be plenty of time for you to get to know them better real soon. Shelly will meet with you later this week to go over your duties.''

The employees said their good-nights and wandered off to wrap up their tasks before going home. Harlan did as he'd promised and gave Shelly and Emily a complete tour of the house, then turned over the keys to both it and an almost-new Ford Bronco that was parked in one stall of the three-car garage.

Shelly decided to drive the Bronco back into town so she'd have transportation, and she and Emily followed Harlan until he turned off to go to his own home.

Even though she had only twelve dollars in her purse, Shelly decided this was a good night to splurge. "How would you like to eat at O'Donald's tonight?'' she asked Emily. "Or maybe Pizza Place?''

Emily's eyes grew wide. "Pizza Place? Really?''

The child's delight at such a simple pleasure almost broke Shelly's heart. She'd been able to give Emily so little...until now. The ranch, the company, the money were all things Shelly could live without. But it was wonderful finally being able to provide for her daughter's comfort and welfare without worrying about every penny.

"Pizza Place it is." Shelly turned onto the main street of Deer Ridge and drove to the distinctive red-roofed building. She parked the midnight blue Bronco and carefully locked the doors. It had been several months since her car had died an untimely death. And never had she owned such an expensive vehicle. She felt like Cinderella going to the ball in a coach that had once been a pumpkin.

They went inside and were seated at a table by the perky teenage waitress. It took Emily several minutes to make a decision from all the options on the menu, struggling to decide between pizza and spaghetti. After they'd placed their order, Shelly wondered if her own eyes held the same excitement and disbelief that was sparkling in her daughter's.

"So, what do you think, Emily? Are you looking forward to moving onto the ranch?"

Emily gave her a look that clearly said her mother's question was ridiculous. But, apparently hesitant to show too much enthusiasm until she knew how Shelly felt, Emily commented noncommittally, "It looks like a nice house."

"Yes, I'm sure it is. But what I want to know is how you feel about all this."

With a maturity well beyond her eleven years, the girl leaned forward and stared intently into her mother's eyes. "I think it's great. It just doesn't seem real, you know?"

Shelly could still barely believe it all herself, so she hoped she could adequately explain it to her daughter. "I told you a friend of mine, who used to come into the diner, gave me a job at the railroad. He knew that you like horses and that I needed a better job so I could make a good life for you and me. He also thought we would take good care of his home, so when he died, he left us his ranch in his will." She understated the full magnitude of the inheritance because she didn't want to overwhelm Emily.

"Where will I go to school?"

Shelly breathed a little sigh of relief. It was a normal-kid kind of question for which she had a quick answer. "You'll be able to go to the same school, but your bus ride will be a lot longer. I'll be home when you leave in the mornings, but I probably won't be back before you get home. But the good news is that I won't have to work nights, so I'll be there with you then.''

"That's great, Mama.'' Emily gave Shelly an apologetic look as she admitted, "I never liked staying home alone all the time, even though you were just downstairs and I was usually asleep.''

The waitress returned with a small pizza and a child's order of spaghetti, which she set in front of a delighted Emily. The conversation ended until the food was all gone. When Emily finally put down her fork and wiped the tomato sauce off her chin, she grinned broadly.

"That was really good. Do you think we can come here again sometime?''

"Sure. Now that I have my evenings free, we'll try to go out someplace for a treat once a week.''

Emily's smile slowly changed to a perplexed frown. "What will you do at the railroad? Will you be riding on trains?''

"No, not every day. I don't really know what I'll be doing yet. I was at my new office today, and tomorrow I'll be meeting all the people who'll work with me.'' Shelly couldn't be more specific because she still hadn't had a chance to get the details of her duties. All she knew was the little Harlan had told her during a quick tour of the offices earlier that afternoon.

"Wow, cool. Wait till I tell the kids at school about this,'' Emily said enthusiastically.

"It's going to require some adjustments on both our parts, sweetheart. It won't all be fun and games.''

Shelly looked up just as a tall, handsome man entered the restaurant with an even taller, blond man. The young waitress immediately approached them, her manner openly flirtatious, and the men responded in kind, joking with her as she led them to an empty table. Their path took them past Shelly's table, and as the men approached, the dark-haired one's gaze fell on her and registered a surprising range of emotions.

She'd recognized him immediately as the man named Jim...yes, the man who'd so persistently pushed into her thoughts while she was trying to work last night...could it have been less than twenty-four hours ago? Her life had changed so drastically since then that it was difficult to imagine.

From the expression on Jim's face, it was obvious he knew her, too. There was a look of surprise, then recognition, then something that faintly resembled panic.

He hesitated, and for a moment Shelly thought he would just walk past without saying anything. Finally he said, "Hi again...Shelly, isn't it?"

She nodded and smiled. "So how did the job hunting go today?"

"Job hunting?" The blond man had also stopped and looked curiously at his companion.

"It went great. They had an opening, and I'll start tomorrow."

"Which department?" she asked. "Coincidentally, I'll be working there, too. We might run into each other."

Again his eyes darkened with what could have been either anger or frustration...or a little of both.

"I doubt that. I'm sure my job repairing the rails will keep me away from the offices." Jim turned to his friend. "Boomer, why don't you go ahead to the table and order for us? I'll be there in a minute."

"But..." the man named Boomer began, but Jim silenced him with a look. With a shrug, the blond man followed the waitress to a table in the rear of the restaurant.

"Did you find a place to live?" Shelly asked.

"Oh, yeah. I bumped into an old friend—" Jim nodded toward the other man "—and he knew of someone who wanted to sublet an apartment. So, I took it."

"Oh. I was just asking because my apartment will be vacant later this week," she remarked quickly. As she noticed Emily's curious stare, she realized she might have sounded too interested in the details of his life.

Jim must have seen it, too, because he leaned forward and held out his hand. "And you must be Emily. I'm Jim. I just met your mother at the Spur."

Emily was clearly fascinated by this man who was speaking to her as if she was an adult. "It's nice to meet you," she said, placing her much smaller hand in his and shaking it solemnly.

"I hear you're going to be the fairy godmother in your school play." His blue eyes twinkled as he flicked a gaze at Shelly.

"Yes." Emily nodded eagerly. "Mama's going to make me a pair of wings and a wand. I have *lots* of lines to learn, too." Emily paused and studied him intently for a moment. "You know, you look exactly like Prince Charming on our posters. He's tall and handsome and has dark hair just like yours."

"I've never been mistaken for Prince Charming before." Jim took Emily's hand and swept into a low, elegant bow. "But for you, Lady Emily, I'll do my best. Any dragons to slay or wrongs to right?"

Emily giggled with delight as she shook her head.

"Well, there's one thing I can do." The twinkle turned to a challenge as he looked directly at Shelly. "I took some drama classes in college. If your mother agrees, maybe we can set up a time, and I'll help you."

"Would you really?" Emily turned to her mother. "Mama, please..."

Shelly refused to admit she'd been outmaneuvered. "We'll see."

Jim gave her a confident smile. "I guess I'd better get over there before Boomer eats all the pizza." He nodded toward Emily. "Good luck with your play." Then to Shelly he added, "I hope I'll see you around."

As she watched him walk away, her gaze drifted from his broad, sweatshirt-covered shoulders down to slim hips and a wickedly sexy butt encased in tight, faded jeans.

Yes, she hoped he'd be seeing her around, too. Maybe it was time she stopped playing so hard to get.

WITH EMILY OFF to school on time the next morning, Shelly had a few moments to stop in at the Spur downstairs and have a cup of coffee before the small moving van arrived to transport their meager worldly possessions to the D-Rail. The diner was almost clear of the breakfast crowd as she entered the side door.

"Good morning, Bernice," she said, pushing open the kitchen door and peeking inside. "Is Pete in his office?"

"Hey, girl, where've you been? You better get in there and calm him down. He had to come in last night

to cover for you. By the way, how'd your meeting go
with that attorney?''

"It went fine. I'll tell you, when you have a few free
minutes. Right now I need to go and make peace with
Pete." Maybe she was being superstitious, but she still
hesitated to tell everyone about her apparent good
fortune. Her mother had always warned her to be-
ware of what seemed to be too good to be true, because it usually was. Shelly walked to the back of the
diner and knocked on Pete's office door.

"Yeah, come on in," called Pete from behind the
door.

Shelly opened it and walked in. "Sorry about not
working last night. Something totally unexpected came
up."

He was engrossed in the sports section of the morning paper and didn't look up. "Well, don't expect me
to fill in for you *every* night."

"Actually, I need to talk to you about that." Shelly
stood nervously in front of Pete's desk, waiting until
he looked up at her.

He must have sensed her concern because his expression softened. "What is it? Is anything wrong?"

"Not wrong exactly. I met with an attorney from
the Texas Pacific Railroad yesterday morning." She
moved a stack of *Sports Illustrated* magazines off the
chair next to his desk and sat down. "Remember that
man, Sam Mitchell, who owned the railroad? Well, it
seems that he left it to me, along with his ranch. They
want me to take over immediately."

Pete's eyes widened and he dropped the newspaper
on the desk. "You're kidding, right?" He stood up
and peered down at her as if trying to detect some sign
that she was making up the whole story. When she

didn't comment, he gasped. "You're not kidding. Shelly that's great. You deserve a break like this. Congratulations." Pete seemed genuinely happy for her as he pulled her to her feet and enveloped her in a friendly hug.

"I'll be out of the apartment sometime this morning." Tears filled her eyes as she thought about how he'd helped her when she was desperate. "I can't thank you enough for all you've done for me."

Pete held Shelly at arm's length with his hands on her shoulders. "If you need anything, anything at all, you know where I'm at. Got it?"

"Got it!" Shelly was touched. Pete was so proud of his gruff, no-nonsense attitude, that his unexpected warmth was a side of him few people saw. With a smile on her face, Shelly left the Silver Spur for the last time as an employee and returned to her apartment to prepare for the movers.

She was in her bedroom, packing her underwear, since she couldn't tolerate the thought of having the movers touch her intimate things, when there was a knock on the door. She glanced out the window and saw a moving van parked near the steps leading up to her apartment.

"You Shelly Lowell?" questioned a tall, thin teenage boy after she opened the door.

"Yes, I am."

"I'm Denny, and Jack's down in the truck. You ready to move?"

"Yes. Come on in." She glanced around and thought how very little space her possessions would take in the moving van. Actually, it would have all fit in the back of a pickup truck. "None of the furniture goes except the portable TV in the living room. It's just our clothes, some books and a few odds and ends."

Denny entered the apartment, looked through all the rooms and then headed back down to the van to get some boxes and packing material.

Shelly resisted the temptation to help, but couldn't keep from hovering nearby as the two men packed and loaded her and Emily's things. It took them less than an hour to pack and load it all.

"We'll take this out to the ranch and unload it," Jack told her as he held out a bill of lading for her to sign.

"Thanks." She handed him his clipboard and pen, then was left alone in the apartment as the men departed.

Shelly turned one last time to look at the apartment that had been their home through the last few lean months. The day she and Emily had lugged their suitcases up those stairs, she never, in her wildest dreams, would have guessed she'd be moving from a place like this to a mansion like the D-Rail.

As she turned to leave, she looked up in surprise at the shadow cast from the doorway.

"Oh!" she gasped when she recognized Jim. "You scared me to death. What're you doing up here?"

"I stopped in the diner to say hi, and they said you were moving out."

She looked at him curiously. Although his words were friendly, Jim didn't sound all that thrilled with her stroke of good luck. Shrugging it off as her imagination working overtime, she smiled.

"Just like that song from the old television show, I'm moving on up. It's going to be strange, but I have to admit that I'm looking forward to living in a real house again.''

''I'm glad I caught you. I didn't want you to leave without giving you one more chance to go out with me,'' he said jokingly.

''That was big of you. And just where were you planning on giving me a chance to go?'' Shelly bantered. It was odd, but every time this man was within fifty feet of her, there was some sort of energy that made her feel vibrant and alive. As much as she wanted to avoid any other complications in her life right now, the thought of spending more time with him intrigued her.

''I thought we might kick up our heels . . . literally. Ever done any country and western dancing?''

''A little. But it's been a long time.''

''For me, too,'' he admitted. ''Hey, I'll even spring for dinner.''

Shelly wondered how he could afford it, since he couldn't possibly have gotten a paycheck yet. But he seemed so confident that she didn't question it. Maybe at the restaurant she could offer to pay half. It dawned on her that, subconsciously, she'd already accepted his offer of a date. As if she was caught in the eye of a hurricane, circumstances were sweeping her along, changing her life. She'd always heard that good things happened in threes. Maybe Jim was one of them.

''Which night did you have in mind for this heel kicking?'' she asked.

''Friday . . . around six?''

''Okay. Why don't you pick me up at the D-Rail?''

''Uh . . . the D-Rail?''

"Oh, you probably don't know where that is." She gave him the simple directions, then added, "Just stop at the gate and push the button."

He nodded and followed her out of the apartment. They stopped at her Bronco, and he closed the door once she was inside. With a jaunty wave she backed out and drove her new truck toward her new job, where she would spend the rest of the day at her new company with her new employees, before heading home to her new ranch and anticipating going on the first date she'd been on in more than a dozen years.

Shelly laughed aloud at the thought that her own fairy godmother must have been working overtime lately. Life just didn't get any better than this.

Chapter Five

"I know it sounds like a strange request, Boomer, but I need to borrow your truck." Jim held the phone a few inches away from his ear as his friend's curious voice literally boomed across the lines.

"What the hell would you want with a pickup truck? That's not your style."

"Yeah, I know. But things come up. Come on... what do you say? I'll even let you have my Vette to drive." A brand-new Corvette for a beat-up old pickup truck. Such a deal. Boomer would be crazy not to take him up on it. Hell, Jim was crazy to lend out his precious car even if it was just for one evening. He'd never even let anyone else drive his baby, much less borrow it. And he wouldn't consider doing it now, except that it was vital to his plan. He couldn't possibly take Shelly out in the Vette. It didn't fit the image of himself he'd created for her. She was expecting someone much poorer.

"Okay." Boomer finally gave in to Jim's persistence, but not without one last jab. "I guess I don't need to know why if you don't want to tell me.... Anyone who'd trade their Vette for old Louise must have a screw loose. Just take good care of her. She's a little sensitive, you know. And fill her up before—''

"Yeah, yeah. I will. Jeez, you'd think I was dating your sister," Jim muttered. "By the way, did you get the heater fixed?"

"Trying to back out of the deal?" Boomer asked, showing the first hint of how much he was looking forward to the temporary trade.

"Just trying to dress right. You know, shorts or thermal underwear. Does it work?" insisted Jim.

"Off and on. If it doesn't stay on, just be patient. It should kick in after a few miles. When you comin' over for it?"

"Just have to get ready and I'll be there. See ya in a couple."

"Glad to be of help. Although, if I knew more about it, I could—"

"Bye, Boomer, and thanks." Jim hung up the phone before his friend could regroup and begin a new attack. He crossed to the patio door and gazed out at the lake. The view from the balcony was one of the things that had sold him on this condo when he'd rented it five years ago. Even though he'd spent as many nights as possible away from this town, it was comforting to have a place to come home to.

Of course, he'd always expected to come home someday to the ranch again. All the best—and worst— memories of his childhood had been there. It was an important part of his heritage . . . until a thief in the night had slipped in and stolen his birthright.

His eyes narrowed as he stared at the wind-whipped whitecaps lapping against the nearly frozen shoreline. Usually the water was calm and relaxing. But, like Jim's own inner turmoil, the surface was choppy and disturbed, its almost clear liquid absorbing the stormy grays of the winter sky.

After a few moments he blinked, then rapidly turned around and looked at the clock on the wall above the large stone fireplace. It was already five o'clock. He was supposed to pick up Shelly at six, and he still had to change clothes and stop by Boomer's on the way to the D-Rail.

Jim took a quick shower and dressed in his near-best country and western dancing digs. As he struggled to put on a pair of well-worn cowboy boots, he wondered how the night would go. Prince Charming on his way to the ball in a borrowed carriage. . . . Not exactly the stuff fairy tales were made of, but it should help facilitate a happy ending—at least to his story.

The dancing would make it difficult to talk, but he was counting on it to lull her into a false sense of security. And it would give him a chance to put the final polish on his planned verbal assault. Then, on their way home, he could get her to admit to things that would make his case. This would be his last chance to get to the bottom of this mess, so he had to make every minute count.

Look out, Shelly Lowell...you're about to be swept off your feet, then dumped back into the cinders where you belong.

JIM DROVE THE FORD pickup to the front gate of his dad's ranch and stopped next to the speaker. He eased down the driver's window, the uncooperative crank groaning a protest in his firm grip. As the glass finally reached the bottom, he pushed the button and waited. When Shelly spoke, chills raced down his spine. It had been quite a while since he'd been to his father's house, and to hear her voice over the speaker raised the hair on the back of his neck.

"Who's there?" she asked.

"It's me," Jim answered with intentional vagueness. He didn't know who might be listening, and there were probably people still working for his father who would know him. He couldn't afford to have his cover blown yet. "Are you ready?"

"Sure am. Drive on up." The gate began opening even before Shelly finished speaking.

Jim shifted into first gear and pressed firmly on the accelerator. The truck leapt forward, choked back, then eventually eased across the metal pipe cattle guard as the gate closed silently behind him.

The drive toward the house brought back more memories than Jim cared to have resurrected. His mother had paid him a quarter for each bucket of pecans he'd gathered from beneath the heavy-limbed trees. When he was young, he and his cousins had hunted Easter eggs around the knobby roots of the trees and in the flower beds that lined the driveway. When he was older, he and his friends had built tree forts and told ghost stories late at night while the moon played peekaboo in the lacy leaves.

And his father had taught him how to drive along this narrow, winding road. *His father.* It all came back to him. He'd been the greatest single force in Jim's life. And even now he was determined to control his son.

It had been difficult enough growing up in the shadow of a local legend. As a child, Jim had listened and learned. But as an adult, he had, after a lot of soul searching and brave giant steps away from the safety and shelter of his home, discovered his own identity.

Unfortunately, that identity had clashed with his father's ideals. Two stubborn men...that shocking will...and, once again, Jim was lost in that tall, powerful shadow.

He came to a stop in front of the door just as Shelly walked out on the porch to greet him.

"Hi, Jim. Have any trouble finding this place?"

"No." He shook his head for added emphasis, then looked around nervously as he got out of the truck. "Ready to go?"

"Would you like to see Sam's...I mean, my ranch? I gave everyone the night off, but I think I can find my way around."

Jim breathed an internal sigh of relief that no one was there who would recognize him. "Sure, I'd love to see it," Jim said as he walked up to her. The gentle fragrance of her perfume filled his senses, and the sparkle in her eyes warmed his heart. He stopped close in front of her, and for a moment he was totally drawn in by her subtle spell. She wore a bright red Western shirt with a sassy row of fringe across the chest and a pair of tight black jeans. A silver conch belt cinched her small waist, and a pair of black suede cowboy boots encased her feet. As a final, perfect touch she'd added a black felt cowboy hat, tilted to a jaunty angle. "You're beautiful," he said.

"Thanks. That's sweet of you to say." She ducked her head, acting as if she wasn't used to hearing compliments.

Usually they flowed easily and mindlessly from his lips, all part of the game of love. But this time his sincerity surprised even himself. "I mean it. You look really great."

Shelly looked up at him, and he was disturbed by the vulnerability he saw in her eyes. This woman wasn't like any of the flirty cheerleaders or sexy jet-setters on whom he'd honed his irresistible charm. It occurred to him that she was going to be very hurt when she found out the truth. Even though it was vital to his plan, he hated seeing the openness in her expression or feel the warmth of her welcome. He wanted to grab her and shake her while warning, *Don't be so damned trusting. The clock's going to strike midnight, and the fairy tale will be over. I'm not trying to fit a glass slipper to your cute little feet. In fact, I'm out to send you back to sweeping cinders.* But he clenched his jaw and kept silent.

"I had no idea what to wear," she added, an attractive pink coloring her cheeks. "Emily helped me pick this out."

"She did a good job." Jim's gaze focused on her lips as they curved into a nervous smile. At the moment more than anything he wanted to taste those lips. He wanted to feel if they were as soft as they looked. Or as sweet. Gritting his teeth with resolve, he thrust his fingers into the pockets of his jeans and hooked his thumbs through his belt loops. He knew with absolute certainty that if he didn't forcibly restrain himself, he would pull her into his arms and let his wayward hands drift over those tempting feminine curves and let his mouth explore her pretty face. He muttered hurriedly, "Uh . . . how about that tour."

They walked into the house almost side by side. As Shelly showed Jim from one room to another, it quickly became obvious to Jim that he knew a whole lot more about the layout than she did. If she'd ever spent much time here with his father, she sure was hiding her knowledge of the place well. Somehow that fact both annoyed and delighted him.

He noticed that his father had changed all the pictures on the walls. While fortunate that there were no pictures of him for Shelly to discover, it also pointed out that, in his father's eyes, Jim hadn't been important enough to bother looking at every day, even in photographic form. More disturbing to Jim was the fact that all the photos of his mother were also gone, as well as a few of the many priceless antiques that had been passed down from his great-grandparents. It was as if Sam had been determined to wipe out any memories of the past, both bad and good.

Had Shelly lived in the house for more than a day, Jim might have thought it was she who had taken everything down. But it was obvious that she'd barely moved in, much less begun the process of settling down and doing any remodeling.

Less than twenty minutes later the tour returned them to the entry hall. As they neared the front door, Jim helped her put on her coat. "So where is this pint-size fairy godmother of yours?" he asked.

Shelly started. "Oh...you mean Emily? She's spending the night with a friend," Shelly explained, then smiled. "You're probably lucky she's gone. She wanted to be here...to check you out, I think." She closed and locked the door behind them.

"You'll have to excuse my truck. It probably isn't what you're used to." Jim tried to sound apologetic.

"Don't be silly. It looks like Cinderella's carriage to me. You should have seen the car we arrived here in. It was so covered in rust, it probably could have been mistaken for a pumpkin." She laughed and added, "I haven't been dancing in years. Can you teach me the latest steps?''

Shelly got into the vehicle and Jim shut the door, shaken by her references to Cinderella. It was as if she had read his mind.... Jim shook his head in disgust at himself, then walked around the front of the truck and slid behind the wheel. He'd known all along what her game was, and he was determined to play his own game—and win. "I'll do what I can. I'm not a very good dancer myself. Now if this thing will start and not turn into a pumpkin, we'll be on our way." He flashed her a crooked grin and turned the key. The engine cooperated, and he eased the truck along the turnaround, then down the drive. The electric eye noted his approach, and the iron gate swung open.

As he passed through it, he was relieved to have pulled off this part of the mission. Now he could return his focus to exposing her real scheme with his father. He still couldn't get over how his father had changed the house and removed all the pictures. Had he done that after he met Shelly? Had he been planning on making her Jim's stepmother? The thought sent chills down his spine.

Hopefully the housekeeper could clear up the mystery of the pictures for him when the time came...and possibly even verify the marriage plans. All that information would help when Jim's case went to court.

"Penny for your thoughts?"

Her voice pierced his musings, and he made a quick snap back to the present. "I'm sorry. Just got lost for a moment. You have a real nice house, Shelly. Real nice. Quite a step up from the apartment."

"It's like a fairy tale come true. One day I'm working in a diner, barely making ends meet and living in a three-room apartment. The next, I'm owner of a huge company, and live on a ranch that would make J.R. Ewing salivate."

"I heard a little about how you inherited the place. Who was the old geezer, anyway?" Jim asked casually.

"He wasn't a geezer." There was a defensive edge to Shelly's voice as she leapt to Sam's defense. "He was a nice, funny, friendly and very lonely man."

He glanced over at Shelly for a moment, then stared at the highway ahead as they sped along toward Kerrville at a shuddering fifty miles an hour. "Sounds like you really liked the old guy."

"Oh, I did. I miss him a lot."

"He left it all to you? How'd he even get to know you?" Jim continued to look straight ahead. It made asking questions easier that way. It was growing increasingly difficult to keep his mind on the business at hand whenever he looked at her.

"Well, that's the unbelievable part. Sam used to come into the Spur every Saturday night around midnight. He didn't always even have money. Sometimes I would pay for his coffee and apple pie or a bowl of chili out of my tips. Anyway, we became pretty good friends over the past six months since I moved here."

"Six months? You knew this guy for six months and he left everything to you?"

"Yeah. Six months. Something wrong with that?" Shelly responded, again with an edge to her voice.

Jim knew he was pushing, but he persisted. "Things must have gone beyond the friendship stage at some point. It sounds like the old guy had plans for you."

Shelly stiffened and turned a cold stare on him. "It wasn't like that. He was a dear old man, and we enjoyed each other's company. But it *never* went beyond friendship."

Out of the corner of his eye, he watched her. Even in the dim light of the cab, her eyes glittered angrily. If she was lying, she was a better actress than Meryl Streep. So, she hadn't slept with his father. Unaccountably a weight lifted off his chest.

He dared turn his head for a full look at her, and his heart did a funny little hippity-hop. *What a strange feeling.* A part of his brain registered the thought while another part wished she wasn't so dammed desirable. Oh, he'd dated lots of women who were more beautiful. But, with Shelly, it wasn't her looks as much as some undefinable something that caused him to want to sit and gaze at her all night long, watching the way her hair flowed around her shoulders like a silken cloud and the flare of her nostrils when she was upset as she was at this moment. He wanted to...

"Uh... it sounds like Sam really cared about you, at least enough to want to make your life comfortable," he said. "Sorry, I didn't mean to imply anything." When she didn't appear to soften, he added, "I guess I was just hoping that you and he hadn't... I mean, that you weren't in love with him or anything. It's one thing to mourn a friend, but something else entirely to mourn a lover."

"Well, Sam and I were never lovers," she confirmed. But her expression had changed as she considered the significance of his confession. "The only man I've ever loved was my husband."

"You still miss him a lot, don't you?"

"I'll always miss him. But life goes on, and I've finally learned to accept it. Somehow, Sam's death put

the past behind me. He's given me a new beginning...another chance."

"I guess the old man didn't have any other heirs?"

"Actually, he has a son, but from what I've heard
about him, he's pretty wild and unreliable. I guess
Sam didn't trust him not to blow it all on wine, women
and song."

Jim felt his jaws clench in fury at the unfair judgment of himself. Sure, he'd done his share of fooling
around, but it was more to let off steam than because
he was crazy and irresponsible. He made himself relax so he could continue his subtle interrogation.

"But how are you going to run the railroad? That's
a tough business."

"I won't try to say it's not going to be a challenge," she admitted. "Obviously I don't know anything about it. But the one thing I do know is that Sam
was dead set against the deal with Mexico, so I'll have
to honor his wishes."

"Mexico? What deal with Mexico?" Jim asked with
feigned innocence. Of course he was very familiar with
the Mexico deal. It had been his baby, his attempt to
show that he had a head for the business, his attempt
to prove his worth to his father. Jim had known Mexico was a gold mine waiting to be discovered. Whoever got reliable transportation established first would
have more business than they could handle.

He'd tried every argument he could think of to push
his father into expanding into Mexico. However, his
father had stonewalled the idea in favor of rebuilding
the lines in the Southwest. Sam had said he owed his
old customers his undivided attention and didn't want
to take the risk with a foreign government.

But Jim hadn't taken no for an answer. In fact, he'd been working on a preliminary agreement when he'd been in Mexico at the time of his father's death. The shock had pushed all thoughts of the deal into the background. Now it was back on his priority list—except he now had a new obstacle in his path. But this one shouldn't be as formidable.

"Surely you wouldn't blindly go along with his decision," Jim commented. "You seem like the type of person who would make up her own mind about things."

"Oh, I am. But I agree with him. The routes in the States made the TPRR great, and we shouldn't abandon them now. There are dozens of small ranches and farms who depend on my railroad for transportation of their crops and livestock. If I pulled the trains out, they couldn't survive."

Lord, she sounded just like his dad.

The drive for the next few miles was very quiet as Jim thought about all she'd said. They were nearing Kerrville's city limits when Shelly spoke.

"I didn't tell you, but I think you look real nice, too." She reached out and touched Jim's arm.

He reached across and gripped her hand firmly. Slowly he pulled it toward his face, turned it over and kissed her palm. "I'm glad you think so. We may not be the best dancers, but we'll look great together."

Shelly smiled. "We sure will, cowboy."

The parking lot of the Yellow Rose was full of pickups, so Boomer's truck would be right at home. Jim found a parking place and pulled in, stopping the truck just in front of what could be a mirror image of Boomer's Louise. There wasn't a Corvette in sight, and Jim was again glad for his foresight. He pulled the key out of the ignition and turned to Shelly with a grin. "Ready for some fun?"

"Yes." Her eyes sparkled with anticipation. She was clearly excited about the evening.

Jim realized he was wishing at least some of that excitement was because she was glad to be with him. *Don't be a fool,* he reprimanded himself. *She charmed your dad, and now she's trying to capture you, too, spinning a web as fragile as dewdrops and as tough as steel.* Trying to ignore the bulge that tightened his jeans unbearably—a condition that was almost constant when he was around Shelly—he opened his door and got out. Shelly sat in her seat and waited for him to open her door.

They walked hand in hand to the front of the Yellow Rose. Around the entrance, a half-dozen cowboys and a couple of women stood at the edge of the circle of light from one of the glaring spotlights mounted on each corner of the huge, aluminum building. A night's supply of empty beer bottles stood in clusters along the top of the short wall that ran along both sides of the entrance.

As Jim and Shelly walked inside, any differences between the Yellow Rose and any of a thousand other beer halls in the country were lost to their senses. The blaring music hammered against their eardrums, and their nostrils were assaulted with the smells of leather, smoke, and stale beer and cheap perfume.

"It's kind of loud, don't you think?" Jim shouted. But he still had to lean close to Shelly's ear for her to hear him.

"Yes, it is," she agreed. Instead of being put off by the noise, Shelly turned and smiled at Jim. "Isn't it great?"

Her enthusiasm was contagious, and he tried to ignore the disgusting smells and deafening sounds as he looked around. Even though it had been his idea to come here, it had been more for effect than a personal choice.

The dance floor was straight ahead, sprawling in a large, fenced-off rectangle along the back wall. Small tables for two, three and four people were scattered all around the room, and the bar ran along the left side where every stool was occupied. As Jim and Shelly stood, looking for a place to sit, the song ended. The couples on the dance floor finished the last few steps of a line dance, shuffled around for a few seconds, then filed out the small gates on each side of the dance floor.

As several cowboys brushed past, their gazes openly admiring Shelly, Jim put his arm around her waist in a sudden burst of possessiveness. How dare they look at his woman that way! A reminder that he shouldn't be having such feelings nagged his conscience. This was his game, and these were his rules. If he starting caring about his opponents he would lose his killer instinct.

But as he pulled her toward him, he could feel her feet shift until she was pressed against him. He had to admit that her body felt good curved against him, and in spite of all his doubts about her, he was proud she was with him. There wasn't another cowgirl in the room who even came close to her unique appeal and beauty. Okay, so maybe he could bend the rules a little . . . just this once, as long as he didn't lose sight of his ultimate goal.

The disc jockey began playing another song, leaning into the microphone to speak over the first few bars. "We're going to slow it down now for a real belly rubber, folks."

Jim tightened his arm around Shelly. "Sounds like the man has a good idea. Would you like to dance?"

"I sure would, cowboy."

Without removing his arm from her waist, he guided her to the dance floor. With his left hand gently grasping her right hand, he turned her around until she faced him. She smiled at him, then rested her head gently against his shoulder. Her beautiful body moved in perfect synchronization with his, acquainting him with every soft curve. Each step he took was mirrored by hers, and he could feel her leg pressed against his with every motion. The song ended much too quickly, but as if he'd bribed the disc jockey, the young man played a second slow song immediately after the first one had faded away.

When another cowboy approached, Jim saw him over Shelly's shoulder and discouraged him with a fierce scowl. She felt too good in his arms, and he wasn't about to let some interloper horn in on his territory. *You idiot,* he chided silently. *You've been home too long. You're beginning to think like a Texan again.* Maybe a trip to the Bahamas would do him good. Or a visit to Aspen for a week of great skiing, wild partying and beautiful women.

Shelly sighed, her breath soft and warm against his neck, tickling his skin and sending electric jolts of desire shooting through him. He rubbed his hand up her back until her thick tumble of dark hair curled around his fingers. He'd never felt hair so silky.

No, he'd stay around here for a little longer. He needed to work on exposing Shelly's plot to get his father to change his will. Besides, she felt too good in his arms. Lately his plans to get to know her better had gone beyond simply discovering her motives. If she was as innocent and honest as she was trying to convince him she was, then making love to her would be a unique pleasure. And if she was the woman he'd originally assumed her to be, it would be a night he'd probably never forget. Either way, it would make putting off his vacation plans worth the delay.

"I haven't had this much fun in a long while," Shelly admitted in a happy, relaxed voice.

"Me, too." Jim realized with surprise that it was true. He didn't have to be the ever-charming, slick playboy that had somehow become part of his trademark. With Shelly he could enjoy the moment just for what it was...a chance to be with her. A little pang of guilt nudged his consciousness, reminding him of the irony of the situation. Never had he been more his real self with a woman, yet she didn't even know who he really was.

The second song brought them closer together, both physically and emotionally. As George Strait's clear, strong voice crooned the plaintive words of "I Cross My Heart," Jim's thoughts no longer wandered to other places or other women. He'd totally forgotten the reason he'd asked her out to begin with. All he knew now was that he didn't want the night to end. She was beautiful, intelligent and interesting, three qualities not normally discovered in one single woman based on his vast experience. Not only that, but she was a great dancer.

The song ended and the DJ began playing a line dance song. The couples swarmed onto the dance floor like ants to honey. Jim began maneuvering Shelly through the labyrinth of moving bodies. When he felt her pulling back, he stopped.

"Let's try it," she said, the green highlights in her eyes sparkling in the artificial lights.

Jim wasn't used to admitting his inadequacies to anyone. So he relied on humor. "Real cowboys don't line dance," he said in a pseudo-stern tone.

"Ah, come on, cowboy," she coaxed. "I promise not to tell your horse. That is, if you even know how to ride."

"That sounds like a challenge if I ever heard one. Well, lady, you bet I can ride. In fact, I could have given Roy Rogers lessons. If I had a horse, I'd show you."

"I happen to have nine...or is it ten horses. You can come over anytime and put your money where your mouth is."

"How about Sunday?" He discovered he was holding his breath, waiting for her answer.

"It's a date." She gave him a flirtatious smile. "Now, about that line dance...."

"Nag, nag, nag," he teased. "Okay, I'll risk life and limb just for you."

They took their place on the back row and shuffled through the first set of steps. All of a sudden the whole group shifted and started moving backward, completely catching Jim off guard.

"Just when I thought it was safe, they try to run me down," he grumbled as he dodged a couple of annoyed dancers. But it was said with good humor. He was actually having a ball. And the sound of Shelly's delighted laughter rang in his ears, heightening his own pleasure. If her story was true, he suspected she hadn't had much reason to laugh lately, and it gave him a certain degree of satisfaction to be the one to bring that light to her eyes.

When they finished stumbling through the repetitious routine with increasing proficiency, they found their way to an empty table toward the right side of the dance floor.

After the waitress took their order, Jim spoke breathlessly to Shelly. "You're a really good dancer, you know."

"Yeah? Why do you say that?"

"You let the man lead. So many women want to lead nowadays. I guess it's all part of the woman's movement."

"Is that important to you?"

"Well, it does say something about how the relationship will go, don't you think?"

She flashed him an impudent look. "If I respect the man, I'll let him think he's leading."

The waitress returned with their drinks. Jim reached into his pants pocket and removed a rather substantial wad of bills. He gave the waitress a ten-dollar bill and motioned her to keep the change as a tip. Sitting down, he slid his chair closer to Shelly's. "Then I guess I can interpret that to mean I have your respect?"

"You're getting there," she replied.

He put his arm around her, and she snuggled into his shoulder. Over the next hour they sat nearly motionless as they watched the other dancers, listened to the music while making small talk, and simply enjoyed each other's company. Jim finally asked, "Would you like to dance again?"

Shelly didn't answer for a moment, then turned and looked at him. "Maybe we could head on back, if that's okay with you." She continued to study him as if trying to read his response to her suggestion.

"That's okay, I guess," Jim said in a reserved voice. He couldn't help but believe Shelly hadn't had a good time and wanted to end the night early. After all, it was only ten-thirty. The joint was just getting warmed up. Even if he drove slowly, he would be dropping her off at his father's ranch by midnight. His *father's* ranch? He realized he'd forgotten all about that problem. These few hours with Shelly had confused the priorities of his heart and his mind to the point where he wasn't sure how he should be feeling about this charade. He knew the longer it went on, the more difficult it would be to explain this to her without seeming opportunistic.

"Listen, if you really want to stay, we will," she commented. "I just thought that we could get to know each other a little better without all this noise and smoke. I don't know about you, but my eyes are burning and my eardrums are numb."

His spirits lifted with remarkable speed at her explanation. So she didn't want to rush the evening to a close, either. "And just how much better were you planning on getting to know me?" he teased with renewed confidence.

"We'll see, cowboy. For now, just cool your spurs." The smile on Shelly's face was not discouraging.

They put on their coats, left the Yellow Rose and went out into the clean cold air of the Central Texas night. A short walk away, Boomer's truck waited patiently, parked between two blood relatives.

"This is probably a pickup truck's idea of heaven," Jim said with a grin as he opened Shelly's door and helped her take that first big step into the cab.

"I'll bet most of these never get within a mile of a cow," Shelly remarked. "I guess it's all part of the macho image."

He had to agree with her there, especially since he'd borrowed this one to convince her he was just a good ol' boy. But he didn't comment as he shut her door, then circled and got into the driver's side.

"Sure hope this old thing starts. She's not too crazy about the cold." Jim put the key in the ignition and after some encouragement from his right foot, Louise cranked up. He turned and smiled at Shelly. "Did you have a nice time?"

She smiled at him. "I had a wonderful time. You're easy to be with. Maybe too easy. . ."

Jim leaned over, and reaching out with his left hand, gently stroked Shelly's cheek. As she looked into his eyes, he carefully guided her to meet him in a long and passionate kiss. Their mouths melted together, moving, searching, clinging. . . getting to know each other as their bodies had earlier on the dance floor. Neither was eager to break the contact, but as their passion increased, it became increasingly clear that this was not the place for such intimacies. When he slowly pulled back, he was amused that they had thoroughly fogged the windows.

Shelly followed the direction of Jim's eyes and noted, "I guess we had a good time, huh?"

"We still are. I haven't fogged up windows like this in years." After a last, lingering caress of her cheek, Jim carefully backed the truck out of the space, drove out of the parking lot and back toward the D-Rail.

Several miles out of town the truck's cab was still bitterly cold, not noticeably warmer than the frigid night air outside. Even wearing a leather jacket, Jim was thoroughly chilled, and he could see Shelly was sitting with her hands between her knees trying to stay warm. "It'll kick in eventually," he said, nodding toward the blowing but totally ineffectual heater. "I sure could use someone next to me to help keep me warm. Interested?"

Shelly looked over at Jim and smiled as she scooted across the torn brown vinyl seat. "If you hadn't been such a gentleman at the Yellow Rose I wouldn't think of it. However..."

"If I'd known I was setting a standard of behavior, I might have come on a little stronger," he complained jokingly. As she snuggled against him, he placed his arm around her shoulders. She took off her cowboy hat, placing it on the seat by the door, and leaned her head on his chest. Her arm was lying gently on his and her fingers idly moved in a circular, unintentionally erotic caress.

Her light touch just about unraveled what thin threads of self-control he still held. As she continued, he lifted his right hand and began to stroke the side of her face. Lightly his fingertips trailed across her soft skin and traced around the curve of her ear. Just as he was ready to pull over to the side of the road and launch into a serious warming project, the truck's heater began to pour out hot air, just as Boomer had predicted.

"Damn...the heater's working," Jim muttered in a soft voice.

"Should I move back over to my side?" Shelly inquired, glancing up at Jim.

"Not on your life. Just sit here and relax. The heater might decide to chill out at any minute."

She smiled and settled back against his chest and continued to softly stroke his knee.

Jim found it increasingly difficult to drive...and also to believe that the erotic dance of her caress was unintentional. The slow circular motions on his knee had graduated to a feather-light movement up and down his thigh. She trailed her fingers along the top of his knee and meandered slowly up to where his money clip interrupted their travels. Then she wandered along the top of his thigh before proceeding back down to the knee.

"I'm really glad we had this night together, Shelly. You're so sweet." Jim could hardly believe what he had just said, but it came from the heart. If she had persuaded his father to change his will, it was easy to understand how she did it. But he couldn't convince himself with as much certainty as he'd had in the beginning that that was a possibility. The more time he spent with her, the more he decided that he'd have a better chance of making a case that his father was incompetent and that she was innocent in all this.

But even then the odds would be stacked against him and Shelly ever dating again. He knew, without a doubt, that she wouldn't take kindly to his ruining Sam's character. And he had no idea how he would explain why he hadn't told her who he was. As he thought about all the options and dead ends that lay ahead, he realized they were only a mile from the ranch.

One more mile and their night would be over. Or would it?

"Just about home, lady." When she didn't respond, he prompted, "Shelly?" Still she didn't move, and he noticed, with a feeling that was both protective and disappointed, that she was asleep.

He was focusing on her with such concentration that he didn't notice the pothole in the road until it was too late to avoid it. With a protest of its squeaky, rusted springs, the truck bounced into and out of the washed-out pit in the asphalt. Shelly shifted, then lifted her head.

"I must have fallen asleep. Where are we?" She stared around them sleepily, trying to get her bearings in the darkness. "Oh, we're almost home."

Home? Maybe for her. Maybe for him tonight. At least he could salvage something out of this awkward and inconvenient situation his father had created. Jim slowed and turned the truck into the D-Rail's driveway. Stopping himself before he automatically reached out and punched in the code, Jim asked, "How do we open the gate from out here?"

"The code number is 0607," she answered, then looked up at him. "I guess I can trust you with it. After all, you could have had your way with me on the way home if your intentions weren't honorable."

Jim grimaced and wished she didn't have the talent for always saying just the right thing to trigger the guilt that was never far below the surface. He opened the window, poked the numbers on the keypad and waited for the gate to creak open.

After he stopped the truck in front of the house, Jim walked Shelly to the front door. The night seemed even colder than before, and he'd never wanted anything as much as he wanted to go inside, light a roaring fire in the fireplace and make wild, passionate love to her on the Indian rug in front of the hearth.

"I make a good cup of coffee. Interested?" Shelly asked, standing on the porch looking up at him.

He knew he shouldn't, but he couldn't resist. "Well, I wouldn't mind getting out of the cold for a minute."

Shelly opened the door and led the way through the front hall and into the kitchen. Pausing just long enough to take off her coat, she prepared the coffee-pot and turned to where Jim was standing by the large window in the back of the house. "I had a great time tonight."

He walked over to her, placed his large hands on her cheeks and looked deeply into her eyes. "Me, too," he said with a sigh, then repeated, "Me, too. I hate for it to be over." He leaned down and pressed his lips against hers. She reached around his waist and pulled him closer, rubbing her hands gently across his lower back. He pressed himself tighter and tighter against her, and the space between them was quickly consumed as his interest increased. He wrapped his arms around her, spreading his hands across the sharp angles of her shoulder blades. Her full breasts flattened against his shirt, and he could feel their nipples hardening in response.

His first impression of her thin figure in the over-size uniform at the Silver Spur had been completely off. She was far more fulfilling and beautiful than he'd imagined. And he wanted her.

Jim's fingers trembled as he unbuttoned the top buttons of her blouse. He slipped his hand inside, the heat of her skin exciting him almost beyond control. He didn't feel any resistance from her when his fingers reached her bra. Feeling like a schoolboy exploring a woman's chest for the first time, he slid his hand under the lacy layer and cupped the fullness of her breast. As he leaned down to taste the soft, warm flesh that was hiding behind its frothy, red covering, there was a knock at the back door.

For a few seconds, Jim and Shelly froze. His gaze lifted to hers, and his blood raced at the raw desire he saw burning in her eyes. "Who could that be?" The words came out more as a moan than a question.

"The only person still here tonight is Baker, my ranch hand. I'd better see what he wants."

Reluctantly they stepped away from each other and she rebuttoned and adjusted her clothes, then smoothed her hair before walking to the door.

Jim, fearing recognition, walked into the living room out of sight as Shelly answered the door.

After a few minutes he could hear the door close and Shelly's footsteps across the tile floor as she left the kitchen. "Where are you, Jim?"

"I'm in here," he said, joining her in the hallway. "What did Baker want?"

"One of my horses is sick. The vet's on the way, but I should go down there to help out. Would you like to come along?"

"Well, I really should be going. Is it still on for Sunday?"

"I'd be upset if you didn't show up."

"I'd be upset if you didn't want me to." Jim grinned, trying to ignore the heated blood still pulsing through his veins. Taking her hand, he walked with her to the front door. He kissed her gently on the forehead, avoiding those delicious lips.

"Good night, Shelly."

"Good night, Jim. Please drive safely."

He turned and opened the door. Once back in
Boomer's truck, he turned the heater off and rolled
down the window, needing the freezing air to cool the
desire she'd ignited within him. He didn't know how
much more of this undercover work he could do
without actually getting under the covers with Shelly
Lowell.

Chapter Six

The afternoon was cool but sunny as Jim, Shelly and Emily rode across the lower quarter of the D-Rail. Because it was Sunday, the ranch help had the day off, so Jim felt comfortable invading the enemy territory he knew so well. In spite of the strain of being in his own backyard, but not being able to claim it, Jim was more relaxed than he'd been since he'd received the news of his father's death.

It felt good to be back in the saddle again. He couldn't remember the last time he'd been horseback riding. It had to have been at least five or six years. But riding was a skill that once learned wasn't forgotten. As soon as his feet settled in the stirrups and the reins were gripped in his left hand, it was as if he'd been riding every day.

Actually, when he was younger, he *had* been in the saddle every day. In fact, he hadn't learned how to ride a bicycle until he was in college simply because he'd ridden his horse everywhere he needed to go. He and his friends had played cowboys and Indians, riding over the scrub oak-covered hills and winding creekbeds.

But Jim knew it wasn't only the pleasure of being on horseback again, but the company who shared his afternoon.

Shelly and Emily rode slightly ahead of him. Even though he'd been tempted to lead, he didn't want to appear to know the trails too well. After all these years he still knew them as well as he knew the streets in downtown Deer Ridge and even the much larger city of Austin, where he'd gone to college at the University of Texas. Nothing had really changed. It surprised him to discover that he really did miss this land that he'd always taken for granted would be his to steward and then to pass along to his children.

In spite of thoroughly enjoying the view of Shelly's perfect, blue-jean-encased behind bouncing on her saddle in front of him, Jim kicked his horse and it galloped up alongside hers. "Beautiful day, isn't it?" he commented.

The determined expression on her face showed just how much she was concentrating on controlling her horse. She nodded and tossed him a nervous smile.

"Relax. You're doing fine," he told her. "That horse has never hurt a fly."

Shelly gave him a startled look. "How'd you know that?"

"Uh . . ." Jim glanced at the horse she was riding. Sampson had to be at least twelve or thirteen years old now, because Jim could clearly remember that the horse had been one of his favorite mounts when he came home for visits before he and his dad had their last and most hostile split. But he knew he'd slipped up, and he had to think quickly to cover his tracks. "Just look at him. He has gentle, intelligent eyes and he only cocks one ear back at a time just to listen to your commands. A horse with a bad temper rolls his eyes and flattens his ears at the least provocation.''

"Oh. I suppose you're right." She leaned forward and patted the horse's muscular buckskin neck, then turned to Jim. "Okay, I'll admit that you more than met my challenge. You obviously have spent a lot of time around horses.''

"I've always loved animals," Jim admitted. "I just haven't stayed in one place long enough lately to have one.''

"I've always wanted a horse," Emily said, already riding with the natural grace of a born horsewoman.

"Well, you have a lot to choose from now. Is that one your favorite?" Jim asked.

Emily nodded enthusiastically. "Yes. His name's Grey Ghost, and I think he's beautiful, don't you?" Her blue eyes danced with delight.

"He sure is," Shelly agreed. Then she said to Jim, "Emily has spent every spare moment in the barn or at the corrals with the horses. She thinks she's died and gone to heaven. I, on the other hand, am still getting used to having animals that eat more in a week than Em and I used to eat in a year." Shelly shifted uncomfortably on the saddle. "How far do you want to go today?''

"Can we go as far as that old farmhouse Baker told me about? He said it was over that little ridge and by a creek." Emily pointed toward a small hill a few hundred yards away. "Is it okay if I ride ahead a little? I won't get off the path.''

Shelly hesitated a minute, then nodded. "Okay, but be careful. Horses have minds of their own and can do unpredictable things.''

"Oh, Mama." Emily shook her head with an exasperation that had been perfected by every preteen since the beginning of time. She kicked Grey Ghost in the ribs, and he jogged forward.

Noticing Jim's attention on Emily, Shelly commented, "She's doing pretty well for a beginner, isn't she?"

"She's a natural." He gave her a knowing grin. "A long, hot bath and maybe a little Epsom salts will keep your muscles from stiffening up."

She grimaced. "I'm aching in places I never even realized I had muscles. I wish I had time to ride every day. This has *got* to be good exercise. It's sort of a rule, isn't it . . . the more something hurts, the better it is for you?"

Jim chuckled.

"I really appreciate you coming along with us today. I don't have any experience with horses, and even though there's a trail, I wouldn't have wanted to go far from the house." Shelly glanced over at him. "I hope we're not keeping you from anything."

"No, I didn't have any other plans. By the way, I make a pretty mean cup of hot chocolate. It gets pretty cold at dusk, so we'll need something to warm us up when we get back."

Shelly looked up at the level of the sun that was still high in the sky, then at her watch. "It's going to take us that long? You sound like you've been out here before."

"Just guessing, Shelly. Just guessing." With that excuse that sounded feeble even to his own ears, Jim nudged his horse forward to quicken the pace and put some distance between them. Hopefully she hadn't picked up on his near slip, but he thought it best that he end the conversation right there.

Shelly watched him, sitting tall and loose in the saddle, as he quickly caught up to Emily. Her daughter, obviously feeling confident of her riding skills, prodded Gray Ghost until she was galloping at a leisurely pace next to Jim. Shelly was satisfied to stay back, watching how happy Emily was and how well she and Jim seemed to be getting along.

One of the things Shelly regretted most was that Emily was growing up without a father. Perhaps she should have more actively pursued resolving that when her daughter was much younger. But Shelly's happiness was important, too, and marrying a man solely on the criteria of whether or not he would be a good father was not an acceptable long-term plan, in her opinion. Love and friendship was important, and she wouldn't settle for less in a long-term relationship.

Maybe she was being naive, but she still believed a wonderful man might enter her life, and they would live happily ever after together. Realistically she wasn't expecting that man to be Prince Charming. Just an ordinary man would do... as long as he was sweet, funny, intelligent and tender, and he truly loved her and her daughter. Was that asking too much of a fairy godmother?

They reached the dilapidated farmhouse in less than an hour. Once it was in sight, Shelly braced her tired legs so her rear wouldn't bump against the leather seat as she kicked her horse into a gentle lope. With her muscles screaming in protest, she caught up with her daughter and Jim, just as they were dismounting outside the collapsed front porch.

Obviously no one had inhabited the place for some time, and the years of neglect had taken their toll. The exterior had gone without paint for so long that the wood retained no hint of any color other than a weary, weathered gray. Rust streaked what was left of the tin roof, and a very mature pine tree grew out of what used to be the middle of the house, a living marker of the time that had passed since a family had lived and loved within those walls.

"I wonder who lived here?" Emily asked, peering curiously in the glassless windows.

Jim leaned over and picked up a piece of broken crockery and rubbed his fingers over the smooth, glazed surface. He didn't offer any sort of guess, but seemed to be extraordinarily interested in the pottery in his hands.

"I don't know for sure, but I'll bet it was one of Sam's relatives," Shelly answered. "Maybe one of the ranch hands can tell us. Remind me to ask them tomorrow."

After exploring the place as thoroughly as they dared, they remounted their horses and rode off along the creek. They circled around until they found another trail that was heading toward the house. Trusting the horses to know the way back to the barn, Shelly would have let them have their heads. But Jim took the lead, moving so decisively, she and Emily automatically followed.

Just as he'd said, it was right at dusk when they rode into the barnyard. And, with the setting of the sun, a bone-chilling cold had settled in, making the idea of hot chocolate sound better and better.

They stopped in front of the barn and were leading their horses inside when a huge coal black German shepherd came charging out. The big dog had made Shelly nervous at first, but, with Baker's help, he'd quickly made friends with both mother and daughter. Baker had explained that the dog had always gotten along well with women and was very protective of them, but could be very aggressive with strange men. When he lunged toward Jim, she screamed.

But instead of going for the man's throat with bared teeth, the dog had rested his saucer-size paws on Jim's shoulders and was covering his face with wet, happy doggie kisses.

"Wow, he really seems to like you," Emily commented. "I've never seen him act like that with anybody else, even Baker."

The smile that was stretching across Jim's face faded, quickly replaced by a stern look as he commanded, "Get down, dog." The dog obeyed, but immediately sat at Jim's feet, still looking up at the man. Jim brushed the dirt off his shoulders and shrugged. "I didn't realize you had a dog."

"Neither did we." Shelly was still shaken by what she thought was a close call. "He came with the ranch."

"Yeah, he belonged to Mr. Sam, but he's been living with Baker ever since...well, you know," Emily said, kneeling down to pet the dog. "His name's Max. Isn't he neat?"

Jim looked down at the dog whose long tail thumped against the dirt in response. "Yes, he's a really *neat* dog."

The dog hugged his heels as they all worked to unsaddle, groom and feed the horses. Jim finished quickly, obviously familiar with the routine, then helped Shelly and Emily with their horses. When all the riding equipment was put away and the horses groomed, fed and watered, Emily led the way to the ranch house, the thought of hot chocolate propelling her toward the kitchen door.

Shelly was tugging at the heavy barn door, and Jim stepped forward to help her. At the same instant he reached out, the door moved, and Shelly lurched into his arms. Automatically, he curbed his arms around her, at first to steady her, but then simply because he enjoyed holding her.

She looked up, her expression startled but not distressed by the unexpected embrace. His nostrils filled with the conflicting scents of leather, horses and a feminine sweetness that was uniquely hers. It was a fragrance more beautiful than the most exotic flowers, finest French perfumes or most expensive wines he'd ever smelled.

The screen door on the back porch squeaked open, and Emily's childish voice floated across the dark yard. "Come on, you guys. I'm starving!"

Even though he longed, more than anything, to pick Shelly up in his arms, carry her back into the barn and make wild, passionate love in a pile of fresh hay, Jim forced himself to take a step backward.

"The hinges need to be oiled," he murmured, trying to regain his composure. "The ones on the barn door, I mean."

"Oh . . . right," she answered, her voice equally flustered.

"And it wouldn't hurt to have Baker look at the back door, either."

Shelly nodded, her eyes wide with what appeared to be excitement and disappointment. At least, he hoped that's what he was seeing there. When her hand slid into his as they walked toward the house, he breathed a small sigh of relief. Not because she was falling under his spell, but because he was falling under hers . . . and it felt so right.

Max tagged along behind, curling up on the back porch when they went inside. By the time they entered the kitchen, Emily was sitting on the stool by the island with her empty cup in front of her.

"Are we ready?" inquired Shelly, amused.

"Looks like I have my first customer. I'd better get moving," Jim said as he shrugged out of his leather jacket and hung it on a hook by the door. He proceeded to show surprising culinary skills as he walked around the kitchen as if he owned the place. First, he retrieved the sugar and cocoa from the pantry, then went to the cupboard to find the right size pan. A little water and a quick stir, and on the stove it went. Jim stood over the stove and without bothering with measuring cups added milk to the brew.

"And now for the secret ingredient," he whispered loudly to Emily as he passed her on another trip to the pantry, where he replaced the sugar and cocoa and took down a large bottle of vanilla. In minutes the concoction was complete, and the cocoa was poured into three mugs and delivered to Shelly and Emily with a flourish.

"Cheers!" he exclaimed as he held his cup high.

"Bottoms up," said Shelly.

Emily sat there silently for a few seconds as she obviously searched for the proper words. "To us," she finally stated with a satisfied smile.

"Yes, to us," Shelly agreed, then took a sip of the steaming liquid. "This is really good."

Jim was clearly amused. "You sound surprised. Didn't you think I could do it?"

"I think you could do anything," Emily piped up, her expression filled with adoration as she gazed at him and drank her cocoa.

Shelly was beginning to agree with that, too. So far, he'd continued to amaze her with his skills and knowledge. His humor and his charm made him wonderful company. And he even got along with animals and kids. Could there be a more perfect man? Shelly felt a strange stirring in her heart. No, she couldn't imagine anyone more fascinating or exciting in the world. If there was, she'd never met him. And furthermore, she didn't want to. She was quite content falling in love with Jim.

Falling in love! Where had that idea come from? Boy, she must be lonelier than she thought. But as she watched him exchange corny jokes with Emily and proudly refill her empty cup with his personal-recipe cocoa, she knew it was true. She was falling in love with this man.

Shelly's hands shook as she lifted her mug to her lips again. The warm cocoa left a heated trail all the way down her throat and into her stomach. It had been a long time since she'd felt warm inside. And now, in a very short time, this man had accomplished what she was beginning to believe was impossible. He'd reminded her she was alive...and a healthy young woman with normal desires.

Desires! Yes, her mind was definitely wandering into dangerous territory tonight. Her gaze had all too frequently focused on his anatomy today as they were out riding. The breadth of his shoulders, the ripple of muscles in his thighs, the strength of his hands as they deftly controlled his spirited horse with the slightest touch of the reins.

She noticed all these things, even allowing her imagination to take it one step further to the memory of those long fingers unbuttoning her blouse and those powerful thighs pressed against her. Dancing with him last night had made her very aware of his body... and how hers reacted to it. And today, even though they'd barely touched, her mind had persisted in teasing her with flashes of how he would look without—

"Do you want it?"

Shelly's eyes widened, and she almost choked on the mouthful of cocoa she'd just drunk. "Want wh-what?" For a few terrified seconds she was afraid he might have been reading her thoughts.

"Do you want the last of the cocoa?" he asked innocently. But his eyes were twinkling, and she blushed, knowing he must have somehow guessed her thoughts weren't quite pure.

"Uh...no, I'm not ready for more..." she managed to answer.

"Yet?" Although his question was innocent, its meaning was clear to the two adults.

"Yet," she agreed, surprising them both.

"Well, if you're just going to let it get cold, I'll drink it," Emily spoke up, totally unaware of the sexual tension that was crackling around the kitchen like lightning in July.

It took a few seconds for Jim to snap out of his daze and break the heated stare that was holding Shelly captive. "Uh...okay." He emptied the contents of the pan into the girl's mug, then returned his gaze to Shelly.

"It was a wonderful day, Jim. Thanks for going with us." Shelly forced the conversation back to less dangerous ground. With the storm of emotions raging inside her, she wasn't sure she could handle more verbal duels tonight. Besides, she suspected Jim had a lot more experience in that area than she. She needed a little time to sort through her feelings.

"It was my pleasure," he said, picking up her cue. "Thanks for sharing your horses. I haven't done that in a long time. I'd almost forgotten how much fun it was."

"Well, I'll reserve judgment until tomorrow morning," Shelly said as she shifted gingerly on the edge of her stool.

"Don't forget the Epsom salts. They'll really help." Jim flashed her his irresistibly crooked grin. "And you know what else would help? A good dinner. Do you have any steaks in that freezer? Next to hot chocolate, steaks are my specialty."

Emily was delighted at the suggestion, and Shelly had to admit that it appealed to her, too. Later, they sat and talked, lingering over their plates long after they were empty.

"How're your lines coming for your play, Emily?" Jim asked.

"I have trouble memorizing stuff, and I have a whole lot to say." Emily shook her head with dismay. "Cinderella has even more lines than I do. I was really glad I didn't get that part."

"Maybe I can help you. I used to read lines with some of my friends in college, and I learned a few tricks that'll help you remember quicker. Is that okay with you, Shelly?"

"That'd be *so* cool," Emily exclaimed. "He can, can't he, Mama?"

"Sure. I'm afraid I haven't been much help." Shelly smiled apologetically. "I've been working so much, and now it looks like the railroad's going to take a lot more of my time."

A strange expression flickered across Jim's face, but quickly disappeared as he turned to Emily. "If you and your mom are free next Friday night maybe we could go bowling and then work on your play afterward?"

"You don't have to do that, Jim. Really," Shelly rushed to say, offering him an easy out if he wasn't truly wanting to follow through.

Jim looked at Shelly, and the twinkle in his eye, more than his words, convinced her that his motives were genuine. "I really want to. I enjoy being with both of you very much."

"Okay, then, we accept. We'd like that," Shelly said, reaching out in Jim's direction.

Jim grasped her hand firmly and responded, "We can go to my place after bowling. It's closer to town, and we'll have plenty of privacy there to go over the script."

Shelly nodded. "It's a date, then. But for now I'd better get Emily to bed. She's got school tomorrow, and I have a big day, too. The beginning of my first full week as an executive."

Emily wasn't thrilled, but she obediently got up from her stool, placed her cup in the sink and said, "Good night Jim. I had fun today. Good night Mama."

Impulsively Emily stopped in front of Jim and put her arms around his waist. He reached down and gave her a big hug. "Good night, Emily. It was fun for me, too."

The girl turned and gave her mother a hug and a kiss on the cheek before heading toward the kitchen door.

"I'll be up in a minute to tuck you in," Shelly called out as her daughter left the room.

With Emily gone from the room, Shelly turned to Jim, who had also slid off his bar stool. He put his mug in the sink, then turned to her. "Well, Shelly. Thanks for a great day."

"It has been, hasn't it? I'll see you next Friday night?" She hadn't meant it to be a question, but it had somehow come out like that. It was important that he confirm it, now that Emily couldn't overhear.

"I'm looking forward to it. I'll call you and we can work out the details."

"Maybe we'll bump into each other at the railway yard."

"Uh...no, I don't think that'll happen," Jim stated. "I'll be out of town on some sort of rail job all week."

Jim circled his arm around Shelly's waist as they walked to the front entry hall. He opened the door, then paused. Neither noticed the cold from the outside sweeping in as Jim gently took Shelly into his arms and gave her a long, deep kiss that left her knees dangerously weak.

"Whew...you're a world-class kisser," Shelly said on a sigh.

"You really know how to flatter a guy, don't you?"

"That was an unsolicited testimonial, not a cheap attempt at flattery," she kidded, not wanting him to see how deeply he affected her.

"I think it all depends on who I'm kissing...." He caressed her cheek and gazed searchingly into her eyes.

"You bring out the best in me." There was a strange expression on his face before he turned and abruptly walked to the truck. Just as he began to get in, he looked back at her and called, "I really like you, Shelly Lowell."

Shelly's mouth stretched into a happy smile. "And I really like you, too, Jim Connors."

Jim sat in the truck, turned on the ignition and waved as he drove off. Shelly, who was still standing on the front porch, arms folded against the cold, repeated, "Yes, I really do."

Chapter Seven

"Good morning, Ms. Lowell. How was your weekend?" Shelly's secretary, Nancy Campbell, looked up from her typewriter as Shelly walked through the doorway to the spacious executive offices.

She knew the broad grin that had been on her face since yesterday would give her away, anyway, so she answered, "Just fantastic. Thanks for asking. Oh, and please call me Shelly." As she crossed the reception area, she hummed Phil Collins's song, "One More Night", but in the doorway of her new office she stopped, and her humming trailed off. She looked around, still in awe of this room.

Floor-to-ceiling mahogany paneling lined two walls, with dark burgundy draperies covering the other two walls that were made of insulated plate glass. A plush, hand-sewn area rug was spread over most of the polished hardwood floor, and some of the most elegant solid cherry furniture she had ever seen was arranged throughout the room. She remembered Harlan telling her that her desk was made of the original wood from the first custom business car on the TPRR line. The brass handles had been crafted from the fixtures on the original club car bar, and a pen and clock set was mounted on a piece of railroad tie that had been whittled down to a scale model of a caboose. Overall, the room reflected the deep reverence of a man who had truly loved the railroad business. Shelly knew that for Sam it would have been more of a life-style than merely a job.

Her gaze went to a large oil painting of a much-younger Sam that was hanging on the opposite wall. The portrait had originally been hanging in the library at the ranch, but Shelly had moved it here on her second day at work. It was somehow comforting to be able to look at Sam and ask him what he would do when she had to deal with something unfamiliar. It was almost as if he was in the room with her...guiding her...encouraging her...believing in her.

"Oh, Sam. I miss our talks. They were so special...." She leaned back in her chair and closed her eyes, letting her thoughts drift back to the last time she'd seen him....

"TEN, NINE, eight, seven..."

"Hurry, Emily. The apple's almost down." Shelly leaned through the serving window and called her daughter who was in the kitchen of the Spur.

"Six, five, four..."

"The kitchen door swung open and slapped against the wall as Emily hurried into the dining room. She was moving as quickly as possible, considering she was holding Clara's hand and practically dragging her along. Shelly motioned for them to join her in front of the television set as Dick Clark continued the countdown to midnight.

"Three, two, one... *Happy New Year!*" he shouted above the bells and shouts of the huge crowd in Times Square.

"Happy New Year, Emily." Shelly gave her daughter an affectionate hug.

"Happy New Year to you, too, Mama," Emily answered. "And thanks for letting me stay up so late." She swallowed back a yawn. "See, I'm not even the least bit sleepy."

Looking over the little girl's shoulder, Shelly smiled at Clara. "Happy New Year, Clara," she said, hoping her voice sounded more excited than she was feeling.

"Yeah, you too," Clara responded with an equal lack of enthusiasm. "I never have understood why those folks in New York all stand out in the middle of the street and watch that silly ball drop down that pole." Clara shook her head with exasperation and added with a derisive snort, "City folks!"

Shelly handed them each a glass of grape juice. "Let's make a toast to our health and happiness in the coming year."

"And hitting the lottery for a million bucks wouldn't hurt, either," Clara commented.

"I'd settle for a raise and a few more generous customers who think a good tip is something more than telling me to have a nice day," Shelly quipped.

Shelly sighed, then lifted her chin. In these first few minutes of the new year, she was counting her blessings... good friends, a clean place to live and a decent job. In spite of the long hours and low pay, she was enjoying her life in this tiny hill-country town. At least she was able to spend more time with Emily.

Their glasses clicked together, the thick, scratched plastic making a hollow thud rather than an echoing ring of fine crystal. But the intent of the toast and the camaraderie of the three females couldn't have been more sincere.

"Whew, this stuff is sour." Clara's mouth twisted into a grimace. "Grape juice is a terrible waste of grapes."

"Maybe next year we'll be able to afford champagne after you've won the lottery," Shelly teased.

"Have you ever tasted champagne, Mama?" Emily drained her glass and looked up, unaware that the liquid had left a purple mustache on her upper lip. Automatically Shelly handed her a napkin from one of the dispensers.

"Oh, once or twice. I remember the day your daddy graduated from law school. Even though he didn't have a job yet, and we were several thousand dollars in debt, we splurged on a night out on the town." She smiled at the memory of the two young, ridiculously optimistic, hopelessly in love people who had found a baby-sitter so they could celebrate what should have been a milestone in their lives. The restaurant had been more expensive than she could have imagined. But she and Billy had been so certain their financial troubles were over that they had splurged, even buying a bottle of champagne on the short trip home. There, their celebration had continued in a more private, intimate way. And now, a whole lifetime away, Shelly was celebrating without him, sharing a bottle of grape juice with their daughter and working the night shift at the Spur.

"You look particularly sad tonight Shelly. Is anything wrong?" Clara asked.

"Sort of. You know that old man I told you about who used to drop by every Saturday night around midnight?"

"That homeless bum you're always saving a piece of apple pie for?"

Shelly gave Clara a guilty smile. She hadn't realized anyone had noticed she'd put aside food for the old guy. He'd seemed so lonely and sad that, from the first evening he'd wandered in shortly after she'd begun working at the Spur, he'd touched her heart. Coincidentally, no one but Shelly had ever actually met him, since Clara's shift usually ended at midnight on weekends, and Shelly took care of the diner all alone until Bernice came on at six for the breakfast crowd.

"Sometimes Sam has money," Shelly responded in his defense. "And usually by then the pie's gotten stale, anyway."

"Yeah . . . right," Clara said, her eyes twinkling. "You were expecting him tonight?"

"I was hoping. I haven't seen him in a couple of weeks, and I'll admit I'm a little worried. We've had some pretty cold nights already this winter."

With each passing Saturday, Shelly had grown more concerned. As odd as it seemed, Sam had become a very special friend. There was something about him that had put her immediately at ease, and she'd found herself telling him more about herself, her problems and her dreams than anyone else she knew. And even as she feared for his safety, Shelly also truly missed those hours together.

Emily had grown bored with changing the channels and not finding anything worth watching at that late hour, so she curled up in the corner booth. The diner was empty except for the three of them, and Shelly saw no purpose in Clara staying there and away from her husband, especially since Shelly suspected Clara was staying later than usual only because she felt sorry for Shelly having to spend the holiday alone.

"Listen, Clara, I can handle it from here. Why don't you go home to John and celebrate what's left of New Year's Eve with him?"

"Are you sure you'll be all right?" Clara glanced at the clock, then back at Shelly.

"Emily and I can handle this crowd just fine. You know how Pete feels about paying overtime," she teased. "Now get out of here. I'll see you tomorrow night." She watched Clara hesitate, then take off her apron and toss it into the laundry basket. "Oh, and wish John a Happy New Year for me."

Clara almost managed a smile as she nodded. "I will. Call me if you get swamped with customers, okay?"

Shelly looked outside at the unusually empty highway. "Yeah, sure. They look like they're rushing here from miles around to spend their evening at the Spur." Business usually was sporadic during the late-night and early-morning hours. But tonight, even the truckers seemed to have someplace better to be.

"Well . . . good night." Clara headed for the door. Stopping for a moment, she turned around and said with a sympathetic smile, "I hope this year will bring you happiness."

"Thanks. You, too." Shelly's gaze was pensive as she watched the older woman walk to her car, get inside and drive away.

As the door shut, Shelly looked at Emily as she lay curled up on the faded orange vinyl upholstery of the booth, and her expression softened. Her daughter had been the source of whatever joy Shelly had had in the past few years. In fact, the child had kept her from completely falling apart.

Shelly got a tablecloth from the linen closet and returned to the booth, where she spread it like a blanket over Emily. She knew she should take the child to their apartment upstairs and put her to bed. But somehow it was comforting to have the company, even if Emily was asleep.

But the little girl stirred and opened her sleepy blue eyes...eyes so like her father's...to look up at Shelly. "Who's going to keep you awake, Mama?" Even though she was only eleven years old, it wasn't at all unusual for Emily to try to take care of her mother.

"I'll be fine. Don't forget, I do this almost every night." She stroked the child's soft brown hair...the same shade and texture as her father's...as she settled back on the seat. She reminded Shelly so much of Billy. At times like this she missed him dearly, even after five years.

The bell over the door tinkled, and Shelly turned around. Her eyes widened with surprise, and a smile stretched across her face as she recognized the tall, roughly dressed man who had just entered the diner. Although his gray flowing hair was a little shaggy, his face was clean shaven. Though he was in his late sixties, his bright blue eyes showed there was a quick, alert mind operating behind that weathered face.

"Sam! Where have you been? You've had me worried to death."

"Hello, Shelly. Good to see you, too," he replied wryly. He walked over to the lunch counter and sat on his usual stool farthest from the door.

Shelly's critical gaze noted a pallor beneath his perpetual tan that hadn't been there before. There was something sad and solitary about him, as if he had no one to care about or who cared about him. "I was about to send out a search party," she said, only partially teasing.

"I didn't mean to worry you." He shrugged as if to dismiss any cause for concern. "I've been a little under the weather the last couple of weeks."

"Are you okay now?"

"The doc says I'm fit as a fiddle. Nothing to worry about."

In spite of his reassuring words, the sparkle in his voice was missing. His lively personality had been a bright spot to her lonely Saturday nights for months. She couldn't even count the hours they'd spent laughing and joking with each other. He always managed to lift her spirits, and she did her best to bolster his, although she had no idea just how drastic his situation might be.

Shelly walked to the end of the counter and stopped at the pastry case, where a single piece of apple pie waited under the warming light. "I saved this for you, Sam. Just like every Saturday night." She picked up the small plate and placed it in front of him, then went to the huge coffee urn behind the formica-covered bar.

"So, how have you been, Shell?" Sam asked.

She placed a steaming cup of coffee in front of him and poured one for herself. "I've been fine. You know how it is. Bills to pay, and I just found out that Emily needs braces. Don't want her heading into her dating years with teeth that could eat an apple through a picket fence," she said with a tired laugh. Although she usually kept her business to herself, somehow Sam had managed to break through her barriers. Time after time she'd found herself filling his sympathetic ears with her hopes and fears and troubles. He knew how she worried from paycheck to paycheck about making ends meet and how that now Emily was getting older, the time between paychecks seemed to be longer and longer.

"In my day few people had braces. Having straight teeth just wasn't all that important." He shook his head. "People put stock in the silliest things when they go to picking out a lifelong mate, don't they? Whatever happened to just loving a person for himself?"

Shelly was taken aback at first, but then realized Sam was just trying to get her going, as he often did. "Well Sam, the competition is stiff, especially in a small town. And love is definitely not blind."

He gave her a sharp, intuitive look. "Is anything wrong? You seem kind of down tonight."

She shook her head, not really able to put her feelings into words. Sometimes it all seemed so hopeless, like a deep, dark hole from which she couldn't quite escape. Instead of voicing her depression, she forced her lips into a smile. "I forgot to wish you Happy New Year, didn't I?" she asked with a touch of embarrassment.

"Yes, you did, Miss Shelly. You should be ashamed." The familiar twinkle danced in his eyes. "You know, for as many months as we've been 'seeing' each other, this is our first holiday together."

"You're absolutely right. We'll have to make a date to do this again next year even though it won't be a Saturday night." Shelly walked around the counter and sat on the stool next to him. "I guess a lot of things have changed since you went courting, huh, Sam?"

He considered her question. "Yeah, a lot has changed. Never really stopped and thought much about it, but we didn't have so many ways to know if someone was pretty or handsome enough. We didn't have television, and movies were sorta rare around here. We couldn't drive to Austin or San Antonio on a whim." Sam paused and stared at his plate for a moment, absently cutting another bite of pie with the edge of his fork. He nodded thoughtfully. "Life was a lot different then. I don't envy parents these days. It was hard enough twenty years ago."

"You've never told me if you have any children of your own," Shelly prompted. She'd often wondered about his family even though he'd never mentioned having one. Maybe it was her imagination, but he'd always seemed to avoid the subject.

And tonight was no different. Sam's expression grew pensive as he replied with his usual evasiveness, "People raise their kids to be good adults, respect their parents and do the right things in life. Doesn't always work out, though."

Shelly propped her chin on her hand and studied Sam's still-handsome face. "Any regrets in your life?"

"Just one. I always wanted a son to follow in my footsteps. But when you reach my age you begin to feel that maybe your footsteps are heading in the wrong direction." Sam took another bite of pie.

After taking a sip of coffee, Shelly asked, "What makes you think you're heading in the wrong direction?"

"Oh, I don't know. Just a feeling a man gets when he feels like he's been fighting everyone around them at every turn." He got up from the stool and walked restlessly toward the window of the café to peer through the blinds. Between the horizontal cracks, the neon sign glowed persistently, sending its message to a nonexistent audience in the dark night.

Shelly rose and walked over next to Sam. "I didn't mean to upset you. We can talk about something else if you'd like. The highway is quieter than usual tonight, isn't it? I suppose all the rich folks are partying hearty somewhere fancy." She felt bad that she'd pressed what was obviously a sore spot with him. Perhaps he'd had a bad marital experience, or maybe he and his wife had always wanted children, but hadn't been able to have them. Or he might have even suffered through the heartbreak of losing a child. She wished he'd share his story with her, so she could somehow ease his pain. He'd certainly helped her deal with her own.

Sam was quiet for a moment longer and then picked up on Shelly's lead. "Yeah, they must be having a grand ol' time tonight all right." Sam grinned and looked at Shelly.

She echoed his smile. "Well, if they'd have invited us we could have shown them how to party. I bet you were a real dancer in your younger days."

"Wait a minute, lady. I'm not dead and buried quite yet. If there was a dance floor here, I'd show you a step or two." Sam turned and headed back to his stool at the counter.

"What's your pleasure, sailor?" Shelly tilted her head and gave him a playful wink. Watching his amused reaction, she sashayed over to the jukebox with an exaggerated sway of her hips. "We have a wide variety of music for your dancing and listening pleasure, sir. And I'm paying!" Shelly reached into her apron pocket and pulled out a handful of quarters from her tips.

Sam's look turned to one of amazement. "Are you serious?"

"You bet I am. After all these months of Saturday nights we've spent together, you owe your friend a dance."

Sam thought for a minute. A smile came over his face as he spoke. "How about 'Chattanooga Choo Choo'?"

Shelly hadn't heard that song in years. She didn't hold much hope that she'd find it on the Spur's repertoire, but she humored his request by glancing through the record titles. She was truly surprised to see it nestled comfortably between Los Lobos's "La Bamba" and Garth Brooks's "Friends in Low Places." She deposited a quarter and punched the number, then turned expectantly toward Sam.

With an ever-widening smile, he stood up and crossed the worn linoleum to where she waited in the open space near the front door of the diner. While not large, it was certainly sufficient for a celebratory dance.

Sam stopped in front of Shelly and swept into an age-stiffened bow. "May I have this dance, lovely lady?"

"You may, handsome sir." Shelly took Sam's hands and followed his lead as he launched into a jitterbug at something less than full speed. But she didn't care about the speed. All that mattered was that she was dancing with her best friend on New Year's morning.

They stepped and turned in perfect sync as if they'd been jitterbugging together for years. He pushed her back, then twirled her in a dizzying spin. The polished floor squeaked and whispered beneath the rubber bottoms of her tennis shoes and the leather soles of his scuffed cowboy boots. Their breathless laughter mingled with the singer's scratchy voice as they continued to dance around the entry area.

"Pardon me, boy—pardon me, boy—pardon me, boy—" The needle hung in the groove, repeating the verse over and over in a halting rhythm that defied any sort of dance step. Sam shrugged, then walked over to the jukebox and gave it a swift kick in the side. The needle squealed across the vinyl, and the song ended abruptly.

"Pete's been talking about getting one of those new CD jukeboxes, but can't justify the expense," Shelly remarked as Sam's arm slid around her shoulders and he walked with her back to the counter.

"I hope he doesn't. Those new-fangled machines are just fancy stereos. A jukebox isn't a jukebox unless it plays forty-fives."

"I agree. But I've heard they don't make forty-fives anymore, which means Pete can't add new music."

"So what's wrong with that?" Sam responded. "It's about time someone recognized that old doesn't automatically mean obsolete."

Sam settled heavily on his stool, and Shelly refreshed their coffee before joining him. He looked tired from his effort on the dance floor but was smiling from ear to ear at her. He'd clearly enjoyed the activity as much as she had.

"Whew, boy!" he exclaimed. "I feel like that old record—all I need is a swift kick to get me moving. I haven't danced and enjoyed myself like that in years."

His weathered voice softened as he focused his lively blue eyes on her. "Thank you very much."

"Anytime, Mr. Sam. It was my pleasure. Remember, we have a date again next New Year's. And next time don't be late," she teased. "You missed our toast. Genuine California grape juice."

"By next New Year's Eve you'll have a man your own age. You'll be out there with the rich people, drinking French champagne, dancing and partying all night long."

Shelly kept her tone light and joking to fit the mood. This was certainly no time for depressingly serious reflections on her financial situation. "I'd better start saving my pennies for a ticket to Vegas. Then I'll have to get lucky. Real lucky."

Sam looked at Shelly for a minute, his expression suddenly serious. "You deserve the best life has to offer. You've got a kind heart, and you've been a very good friend to me. You know, the older I get, the fewer friends I have and the more I realize what they're worth. All the money in the world can't make up for being alone."

Her eyes filled with tears. "Yes, Sam, being your friend is worth more than money. I don't think you realize how you've made my life brighter by your weekly visits. I wouldn't have traded tonight for anything in the world."

"Neither would I, Shell." Sam's smile was wistful. "Neither would I."

SHELLY WIPED AWAY the tears that had streaked down her cheeks. Yes, Sam had known he wouldn't be around much longer. And he'd already set the wheels in motion to change her life forever. If only she had known.

But he must have believed her when she'd told him how much his friendship meant to to her. After all, he'd trusted her with all the things that were most important to him—his beloved ranch and his equally treasured railroad. He must have believed she could handle the challenge.

Shelly wished she could be so confident. She leaned forward and stared, with a certain degree of trepidation, at the stacks of papers overflowing several baskets on the desk's shiny surface.

"Nancy, please come in here," Shelly spoke into the intercom.

"Yes, Ma'am?" the attractive young woman asked as she entered the office.

"Harlan said the executive committee was going to meet this week, but he didn't tell me what day. Do you know when it's scheduled and what's on the agenda?"

"Sure do. The note's right here." Nancy handed Shelly an interoffice memo. "I took it off your desk this morning to make a copy for my files. Sorry."

"No need to apologize." Shelly scanned the paper, then grimaced. "The meeting's this afternoon. Please get Harlan on the phone. I need to talk to him as soon as possible. I want to be ready when this Mexico thing comes up for discussion."

"I'll see if he's available." Nancy hurried from the office to place the call.

A few seconds later the intercom buzzed, and Shelly punched the button. "Yes?"

"I have Mr. Dickerson on line one, ma'am."

"Thanks." Shelly punched the blinking button and picked up the receiver. "Harlan? How're you doing today?"

"Fine, Shelly. Just fine. What can I do for you?"

"I need to find out where we stand on this Mexico line expansion project. Can you fill me in?"

"Well, as you know, Sam was dead set against it. On the other hand, his son, who just happens to be TPRR's second largest stockholder, has pushed this from day one. Tell you the truth, Shelly, our lack of commitment to either rebuilding the western branch lines or expanding into Mexico has us falling further behind the competition every day."

"How so?"

"Several other railroads are courting the Mexican government for exclusive rights into their country. If we don't get there now, we may never get the opportunity to do business there."

"I understand that's where Sonny was when his father died," Shelly commented.

"Yes, he was. I suppose he was trying to keep the deal alive until we made a decision."

"And when do I actually get to meet this prodigal son?"

There was a slight pause before Harlan answered. "I'm not sure. I haven't seen him but once since he got back. But you can be sure he'll show up at the meeting."

"Well, I have to stick with Sam's wishes on this, Harlan. He trusted me with his legacy to do the right thing, and I can only assume he knew more about the issue than anyone else. So, how do we handle Sonny?" The still-invisible Sonny was becoming a royal pain as she tried to do her job in the way she thought Sam would want it done.

Harlan was again silent for a moment as he obviously considered how to phrase his response. "He's not a happy camper right now. He sees you as his personal nightmare and will stop at nothing to undo what Sam's will did to him. I guess that's pretty clear, isn't it?"

"Clear enough. How do you suggest I handle the executive committee meeting, then?"

"Even though time is of the essence, if I were you, I'd postpone any discussion on this until you can get your feet on the ground."

"Good advice. I'll have Nancy contact everyone and reschedule the meeting for next Monday. That should give me the time to meet with everyone and get the facts and figures I need to hold my own."

"Good luck, Shelly. Even though neither of the Mitchells would admit it, Sonny's a chip off the old block. He can be stubborn and hard to deal with when he wants to be."

"Maybe we should create a diversion to calm him down," Shelly said, half joking. Frankly, at the moment, she'd appreciate anything that would avoid an ugly confrontation with a disinherited son.

"That may not be necessary. Rumor has it he's found himself a girlfriend. His best friend says he's never seen him so happy. Maybe your timing is right."

"Well, we'll know in a week, won't we? Thanks, Harlan. You're a big help, as always."

Shelly hung up the phone. "Nancy, can you come in here again, please?"

The secretary entered the office with her notebook in hand. She sat on one of the padded leather chairs in front of Shelly's desk and looked expectantly at her employer. "Yes?"

"Please contact everyone and reschedule the meeting for next Monday afternoon." Shelly hesitated, then asked, "Do you know Sonny?"

"Mr. Mitchell's Sonny?"

"Yes."

The secretary shrugged. "I don't know him well. He didn't drop by Mr. Mitchell's office very often, and Mr. Mitchell rarely mentioned him."

Shelly frowned thoughtfully. "If I was going to try and win a debate with him, how would I go about it?"

"Well, I've heard he's always been a lady's man, but I don't think he'd be attracted to you."

Nancy must have realized immediately how that sounded because she hurriedly amended, "Oh I didn't mean it that way. I meant that I've always heard that Sonny only has girlfriends who can do something for him . . . if you know what I mean. They're more like trophies than relationships. He has quite a reputation around here as a playboy, and you're too . . ." She looked away as if too embarrassed to go further.

"I think I know what you mean. Thanks, Nancy. You've been a big help. That'll be all for a while. I'm going to try to look over some of this paperwork, so I'm sure I'll have a lot more questions later."

Nancy got up and left. Shelly leaned over and checked out the panel of buttons on the corner of the credenza. She pushed the one labeled Drapes, and the mechanism quietly began opening the full-length satin draperies. After the heavy material cleared the glass, offering an unobstructed view of the railway yard and the rolling hills beyond, she walked to the window and looked down, surveying Sam's empire.

Surely Sam had known his son wouldn't give up without a fight. And clearly Sonny was someone to be reckoned with.

But she wouldn't do it on his terms. She'd been a victim of circumstances ever since her husband's untimely death. Now that her destiny had changed, she refused to let anyone take advantage of her ever again. Sam had believed in her, and she wouldn't let him down. She was in control now, and she would deal with Sonny on *her* terms.

Chapter Eight

"Did you see that? I got a strike!" Emily jumped up and down in front of the alley, then galloped back to the row of chairs where Shelly and Jim sat, waiting for their turns.

"Good shot, Emily!" Jim exclaimed.

Shelly, applauding in the background, added her words of enthusiasm. "Way to go, honey." Turning to Jim, Shelly whispered, "I've never had the time or money to take her bowling before. This was a good idea."

Jim glanced up at the computer graphics displaying Emily's strike on the television screen above the lane. "You used to be able to learn how to add by keeping score. I haven't been bowling since they put in these new computerized scoring systems." Jim gave Shelly a mischievous grin. "My scores were much higher when I added it myself."

"I bet they were." Shelly laughed. "I guess now you're going to tell me that real cowboys don't bowl, either."

"Oh, they bowl . . . but they never strike out."

Shelly rolled her eyes. "That sounds like a Texas-size ego if I ever heard one."

Jim shook his head. "Texans don't brag. They don't have to, because it's all true."

She groaned and got to her feet. "I think I'd better bowl before the you-know-what gets too deep in here and ruins my bowling shoes." She picked up the nicked black "house" ball and lined it up. Her aim wasn't as accurate as Emily's, only knocking down seven pins. But then, her mind wasn't really on the game.

Shelly sneaked a glance over her shoulder at her daughter and Jim sitting together and chattering about the little girl's bowling skills. It was amazing how quickly Emily had become attached to the man. Maybe she was desperately searching for a father figure. Or maybe she simply thought he was a terrific person... just as her mother did.

They continued bowling until they finished the game. Jim, in spite of his handicap of not being able to boost his score, still won, with Emily barely beating Shelly to come in second.

"Are you ready to practice your lines?" Jim asked Emily.

"Well, to tell you the truth, I'd rather stay here and bowl." Emily was already standing, preparing to take her turn beginning a new game.

"You volunteered for the part, so you'd better get your lines memorized," insisted Shelly. "The play is less than three weeks away."

After returning their balls to the rack and shoes to the counter, Jim, Shelly and Emily left the bowling alley arm in arm. Within a few minutes they were pulling up to Jim's apartment. Jim parked the truck in front of a one-car garage and motioned that Shelly should park in the visitor's area on the other side of the driveway. They got out of their trucks and walked around to the front door.

"You were lucky to find this," Shelly commented as she looked out on the lake that shimmered in the moonlight. "It's so beautiful and peaceful here...a far cry from the apartment we just moved from."

"Yeah, it's a nice place."

"When's the owner coming back?"

"Uh...I'm not sure. It could be quite a while." Jim inserted his key in the lock and opened the front door, flipped on the light inside, then stood aside to allow them to enter first. "Ladies..."

"He's such a gentleman, isn't he, Mama?" Emily swooned, clearly impressed as she walked past Jim and Shelly.

"He certainly is. A real gentlemen," agreed Shelly.

Jim leaned over and boldly whispered into her ear, "You wouldn't be saying that if Emily wasn't here with us, lady."

Shelly glanced up at him. "Do you always get your way?"

"Only when it's important," he answered. "And *you* are important to me."

She had no idea how to respond to that, but her heart fluttered in her chest at the implication that she might actually mean something to him. For a few seconds her thoughts drifted to the possibilities of what might happen if Emily weren't with them. Would she...? Would he even want her...? With a shake to clear her head, she stepped across the threshold and followed Emily into the large family room.

The apartment was nicely decorated in shades of dark teal blue and black, accented with lots of glass and brass. A little masculine, as could be expected, but everything was picked up and put in its place, something she hadn't expected. Shelly walked around looking at the artwork displayed on the walls. "Nice collection."

"Oh, yeah, it's taken years to accumulate." Jim followed her gaze around the room, then quickly said, "Wish it was mine. This guy has a lot of money, but doesn't use this place all that often. More of a hunting getaway during the spring and fall."

"Must be nice to have that much money."

"You do," he reminded her in a low voice.

"Oh, I guess I do." She shrugged almost apologetically. "I still can't get used to it. Last month I couldn't afford a horse poster Emily wanted. And now I could buy a Remington . . . or two."

"Or two thousand," Jim amended. "With all the money you inherited, you could buy a museum."

Shelly gave him a sharp look. "How do you know how much money I inherited?"

His expression never changed as he replied, "I've seen your ranch and your company. I can only assume there was some money in the bank, too."

Although his answer didn't completely satisfy her, she decided she was being overly suspicious. After all, even if he was after her money, she was smart enough to go into any relationship with him with her eyes wide-open. Besides, he just didn't seem like the type who would take advantage of a woman. Like Emily said, he was a gentleman.

Shelly looked around curiously.

Jim, noticing her interest, asked, "Would you like a tour?"

"Sure."

It didn't take long to walk through the three bedrooms, kitchen and dining room. When they returned to the family room, Jim took a long fireplace match and lit the paper and kindling in the stone hearth. The dry chips of wood ignited quickly, and the popping sound of the fire filled the room. He looked around at Emily. "Are you ready to begin?"

"Mama, do I have to?" she asked, not wanting to work when she was having such a good time.

"Now, Emily, Jim's been nice enough to offer to help, and you certainly need the practice. Come on. It'll be fun."

"Okay..." Emily picked up her notebook and moved over to sit next to Jim on the couch. Shelly sat down on the other side of Emily.

"You're the fairy godmother, right?" Jim asked.

Emily nodded unenthusiastically.

"Shelly, you can be Cinderella, and I'll be Prince Charming," he continued.

"Typecasting," Shelly remarked, flashing him a teasing smile.

Emily immediately took control. "Okay, Mama, you kneel down in front of the fireplace, and the prince isn't in this scene, so Jim can play all the parts of the evil stepmother and stepsisters."

Jim hunched his shoulders and croaked in a high-pitched voice, "Nibble, nibble little mouse...who's that nibbling on my house..."

"That's *Hansel & Gretel,* not *Cinderella,*" Emily stated with childish exasperation. "Here's the script. Mrs. Selby said *no* fat-lipping."

Jim gave Shelly a puzzled look. "Uh...I think she meant *ad-libbing,*" Shelly gently corrected.

"Okay," Jim agreed, not quite able to mask a smile. "I'll be right back." He left the room and returned a few minutes later, wearing a bathrobe over his clothes. He'd also wrapped a bath towel around his head. "I'm ready, dearies," he said, again using the higher voice.

Emily laughed with delight. She glanced around the room, then pulled a wooden spoon out of the ceramic holder near the stove in the open kitchen area. "This will be my wand," she announced, waving it in the air. "Okay, let's go."

Shelly began pretending to sweep the cinders out of the fireplace, and Jim stalked into the room.

"This house is a mess, you lazy girl," he complained, enthusiastically getting into his role. "Hurry, I need you to iron my ball gown for tonight."

Shelly cast him an amused look. "But Stepmother, I've been working since before dawn, and I'm so tired."

"You ungrateful creature," Jim cried shrilly. "I give you food and a roof over your silly head, and all you do is complain. I should kick you out in the cold."

"Oh no, don't do that, Mother," Jim said, leaping to one side and taking on the role of one of the stepsisters. "Who would wash my clothes?"

Jim jumped to another position and assumed the primping posture of the second stepsister. "And who would fix my hair for the ball?"

Shelly wiped her hand across her forehead wearily. "I wish I could go to the ball."

Jim cackled loudly. "You? Go to the ball? Don't be a goose."

They continued acting out the scene with Emily directing until the stepmother and stepsisters, all in the personage of Jim, left for the ball, and it was time for the fairy godmother to put in her appearance. Emily frowned and whispered to Jim, "I need a ball gown and some glass slippers."

Jim considered her request, then nodded. "You get busy turning the mice into horses and I'll find a dress and some slippers."

Emily and Shelly continued the scene until Jim returned with a sheet and a ragged pair of tennis shoes. "These are the best I could do on short notice," he said.

Shelly tied the sheet around her waist for a skirt and slipped her feet into the oversize shoes. "Oh, thank you, fairy godmother," she said to Emily, but cast an exasperated look at Jim. "I could dance all night in these beautiful glass slippers."

"You can dance all you want, but you must remember one thing," Emily admonished in her best fairy godmother tone. "You *must* leave before the clock strikes midnight. That's when the magic will end and everything will change back to the way it was."

"I'll remember," Shelly promised.

The rehearsal continued until Shelly arrived at the ball. Jim bowed low in front of her, just as he had when he'd first met Emily. "May I have this dance?" he asked.

Emily "fluttered" around the room, waving her wand as Jim took Shelly in his arms and led her in a clumsy waltz. Shelly's feet didn't come close to filling Jim's shoes, and her movements were anything but graceful.

"Having trouble with your slippers, Cinderella?" he teased.

"Now I know how a clown feels," she muttered, tripping for the dozenth time as the toes crossed.

"Then let's try it this way. Put your arms around my neck." She gave him a curious look, but complied, and he, with what appeared to be little effort, wrapped his arms around her waist and lifted her off the ground. Holding her tightly against his body, he twirled them around the room.

"I think we're dancing a little too close," Shelly said breathlessly, even though it was Jim who was expending all the energy. "What will my wicked stepmother say?"

Jim chuckled and gave her a conspiratorial wink. "Trust me. I'm closer than you think to your stepmother." He hugged her even tighter and swirled her in a dizzying circle.

"Dong, dong, dong..." Emily's voice chimed.

Shelly buried her face in the curve of his neck to keep her equilibrium. Instead of steadying her, the movement made her feel even more shaky as she became increasingly aware of just how closely meshed their bodies were. Her breasts were flattened against his chest, and her abdomen rubbed against his. But more unsettling, the intimacy of their impromptu dance was stirring feminine feelings deep within her.

"Dong, dong, *Dong*..."

"I think we should practice this play over and over until..." Jim murmured huskily in her ear. It was evident from the hardening bulge pressing into her that he, too, was affected by the moment.

"Dong, *Dong, Dong!*"

"Until we embarrass ourselves in front of my daughter?" Shelly finished the sentence for him.

Jim gave a startled look in Emily's direction, as if he'd completely forgotten she was there. He rubbed his cheek against Shelly's hair, and his muffled moan was more eloquent than words.

"*Dong! Dong!*" Emily practically shouted the final warning.

"Oh...r-right," Shelly stammered, loosening her arms and sliding back down to earth. For a few moments she'd actually felt like Cinderella, wrapped in the loving, protective arms of the most wonderful man on earth. But this was just make-believe—and she'd be wise to remember they were merely acting out parts. She pushed away from Jim. "I've got to go," she said, returning to the scripted dialogue.

"Please stay," Jim whispered as he looked deeply into her eyes.

Shelly's mouth opened, then closed, unable to recite the next sentence. Jim had sure missed his calling, because he was one heck of an actor. She could have sworn he meant every word. *It's just a play...it's just a play...* she repeated to herself, trying desperately to get back into the role. "I must leave before—" she said aloud. She turned and fled, with more urgency than absolutely necessary, leaving behind, quite by accident, one of Jim's oversize tennis shoes.

"*Dong!*" Emily waved her wand enthusiastically, then clapped her hands. "That was terrific."

Shelly turned, and her gaze met Jim's across the area that had somehow transformed from a magical ballroom back to a den.

"Yes, it was," Jim agreed, but the heat that shimmered in his blue eyes like a haze over a hot highway was sending Shelly a private message.

A fresh wave of desire washed over her, and it took all her willpower not to return to the powerful magnetism of his arms. "I need a drink of water," she managed to say and fled to the kitchen.

"Sorry. I've been a terrible host," Jim said, an apologetic expression on his handsome face. "How about some wine...and a soft drink for you," he added to Emily.

They took a short break, then finished the second act of the play. But the spell had been broken, and the rest of the rehearsal went smoothly. Emily couldn't keep from giggling at Jim's hamming up his parts. And even Shelly admitted he was the most charming man she'd ever met, when he made them all laugh as he pretended he couldn't wedge his huge tennis shoe onto her foot.

But as she stumbled over her last lines, Emily began to yawn. After the imaginary curtain closed on their production, she curled up on a corner of the couch and snuggled into the pile of cushions on the plump, modern-design sectional couch. "I'm tired, Mama. Is that enough for tonight?"

Shelly looked at the large mantel clock just as it began to chime eleven. "I suppose that's a good start, honey. You did great."

"Emily, after you've had time to memorize the lines a little more, we'll do this again. Okay?" Jim offered. He gave Shelly a quick, intimate glance that told her he was looking forward to another dance.

"Okay, Jim." Emily yawned again, and her eyes drifted closed as she murmured, "Thanks for helping me."

"Yeah, thanks," Shelly said before she added with genuine reluctance, "We'd better be going now before I have to carry her out to the car. She's going to a slumber party tomorrow night, so she'll want to be wide awake for that. Her friend Jennifer's mother has my sincerest sympathies." Shelly shook her head. "Imagine eight giggly girls staying up all night and talking about heaven knows what."

"Boys, of course," Jim replied.

Shelly's eyes widened as she glanced at her daughter in horror. "Oh no, not yet. She's still a baby."

"She's eleven, isn't she?"

"Yes, but—"

"How old were you when you first started noticing boys?" Jim asked with annoying male logic.

Shelly's expression grew even more horrified. "Eleven. Uh-oh. It's about to start, isn't it?"

"'Fraid so." Jim actually laughed, offering no comfort at all.

"Well, I guess I'd better take her along now," Shelly said with a perfectly straight face. "I've got to figure out how I'm going to lock her in the house for the next seven years. Lord, I'm feeling old right now."

One corner of Jim's sexy mouth lifted into an appealingly crooked grin. "For an old babe, you've sure held up well."

"Was that supposed to make me feel better?"

"No," he answered as he took a step closer and pulled her into his arms again. "But this is..." He leaned closer so that his words heated her lips just before his mouth did. This time the tip of his tongue dared to tease the tender inside curve of her lips, causing them to part in anticipation. But he didn't take advantage of her subtle invitation. Instead, he let his kisses trail up her face to her nose, her eyes and finally, in farewell, her forehead.

Jim helped Shelly on with her coat, gathered the drowsy Emily into his arms and walked them to the

Bronco. After the two females were seated and belted in, Jim stepped back and called, "Good night, Shelly. Thanks for coming over. And good night, Emily."

The little girl grunted an unintelligible response, but Shelly gave him a regretful, "Good night Jim." She added in a whisper, "I think I'm..."

"You're what?" Jim prompted when she couldn't bring herself to finish the sentence.

She ducked her head and pretended an intense interest in inserting the key in the ignition and starting the engine. "Nothing. I'll talk to you later this weekend?"

"Hope so." He backed away from the Bronco and waved goodbye.

As she began the drive home she thought about what she had almost said. *I think I love you.* She still couldn't believe it herself, so how could she dare voice her feelings to him? But it had been long enough since her husband had died, and Jim got along so well with Emily. This might have happened quickly, but it felt right.

THE BRIGHT LIGHTS, meager though they were, of the city of Deer Ridge lit up Main Street as Shelly drove slowly through town. She'd left her ranch only thirty minutes earlier, alone, with plenty of money in her purse and absolutely no plans. It was Saturday night, and her daughter was safely tucked away at her friend's house. For the first time in years Shelly felt free to do as she wanted... *anything* she wanted.

Too bad she couldn't think of something.

It must be because she was out of practice. For the last twelve years, her life had been so focused on making enough money, first to support her husband as he finished his education, then taking care of him when he got sick and later to support her daughter and herself, that she hadn't had much free time to kill. So until tonight, what to do with her free time hadn't been an issue.

As she circled at the end of town and headed back through, no matter which direction she tried to steer her thoughts, they insisted on turning to Jim.

Jim. What was she going to do about Jim? It was too soon to fall in love, but he had brought so much excitement and happiness into her life already. He seemed perfect. Maybe it was time she made a choice. Be alone or take a chance on love.

Shelly slammed on the brakes as the only stoplight in the center of town turned red. She'd been so distracted, she'd hardly noticed it until she was already halfway into the intersection. Nervously, she glanced around, hoping the one cop on duty at night wasn't in the vicinity. But then, at this time on a Saturday night, he was probably at the Silver Spur enjoying a greasy hamburger and a cup of coffee and exchanging insults with Clara.

Just as suddenly as she'd stopped, she realized that just up the road to the right, only about a mile from this very spot, was Jim's apartment. Maybe tonight was the night to find out if he felt the same way she did, and if there might be a future for them. There would be no ranch hand or fairy godmother wanna-be to interrupt them. Maybe it was time they had a long talk about something other than railroads and fairy tales. Maybe tonight was the night she'd find out if her own story might have a happy-ever-after ending.

As she impulsively flicked on her right turn signal, she wondered if he would mind a surprise. She changed her mind a dozen times during the short drive to his apartment building. But she continued on until she parked her car in the parking lot near the door of his apartment. She looked around but didn't see Jim's truck, although there was a black Corvette parked in his driveway. Maybe the truck was parked inside the garage. Or maybe he wasn't home. She paused as another thought struck her. Maybe he had a visitor... a *female* visitor.

But at the moment it didn't matter. Her nerve was up, and now was the time to knock on the door and find out if she was the only woman in his life or just one of many. She pulled her Bronco into the same space it had been in last night, parked it and got out.

She walked around to the front door and knocked. Inside she could hear the sounds of country and western music on the stereo, playing a slow song... a romantic song that she recognized as the same George Strait tune they'd danced to at the Yellow Rose. Her fears increased that he might be entertaining another woman. She swallowed a lump that had suddenly risen in her throat and started to turn away. Perhaps she should leave and avoid an ugly scene. Maybe she wasn't ready for this giant step, after all....

But before she could take a step, the door opened.

"Shelly!" Jim exclaimed with obvious surprise. He was wearing only a pair of tight jeans with the top button unfastened, leaving a tantalizing view of dark hair curling around his belly and trailing into the vee opening of his pants. His hair was tousled, falling across his forehead in appealing disarray.

She'd never seen him so casually dressed ... or, in this case, undressed. He looked as if he'd been on his way to the shower... or perhaps just out of bed. Again it struck her that he might not be alone. Perversely she wanted to know... and yet she didn't....

"Is this a bad time? I can come back another day." The attack of nerves that had been threatening chose that moment to take over completely. If Jim hadn't reached out and wrapped his strong fingers around her arm, she might have chickened out completely and fled back to her Bronco.

"No, not at all. Please come in. I was just thinking about calling you and seeing if you'd like to take in a movie or something." Jim stepped back into the apartment and, with gentle pressure on her arm, left her no option but to follow.

Hearing the door close behind her, she turned toward him. "I was out driving and found myself in your neighborhood. I... I just thought..."

Jim placed his finger over her lips. With his left hand he pulled her closer to him and then replaced the pressure of his finger with the warmth of his lips. Even if she wanted to speak, he efficiently prevented whatever weakened objections she may have had. Even though he didn't wrap his arms around her, she could feel the heat of his almost-naked body radiating across the fraction of an inch that separated them. Her fingers itched to stroke his smooth tanned skin and tangle in the nest of curls that spread across his chest.

When he finally pulled away, there was a dazed look in his eyes. "Wow... you really pack a wallop, ma'am," he drawled, his voice husky with emotion.

Shelly just blinked, temporarily incapable of speaking. All she knew at that moment was that she had never, even with Billy, felt such passion and raw, raging desire. It frightened her... and filled her with anticipation. Surely such deep feelings were love. And the man who generated those feelings had to also be in love with her.

Her heart soared. Suddenly all the years she had gone without love seemed to expand like a hot-air balloon, suffocating her with their enormity. Life was passing her by. She was almost thirty years old, and except for a beautiful daughter, she had not done anything with her life other than merely survive. It was time she listened to her heart and made the most of every moment.

"We could go out and see that new Mel Gibson movie at the Longhorn. Or we could stay in and see what's on cable," Jim offered after taking a step backward as if he couldn't think clearly unless there was a physical distance between them. He walked over to the coffee table, picked up the *TV Guide* and began flipping through it. "I think there's an old Peter Sellers movie on...one of the Pink Panther series..."

Shelly moved forward, stopping just inches from him. She took the magazine from his hands and tossed it back on the table. "Why don't we just talk?"

There was a pained expression in Jim's eyes. Nervously he dragged his fingers through his dark hair, rumpling it even more than it had been before. "On second thought, I think we'd better go out...I'm not sure if I can keep my hands off you if we stay." The muscle in his jaw flexed as he tried to stifle a groan. "Frankly, lady, the last thing I want to do with you right now is talk."

Her eyes met his with a boldness she didn't know she possessed. "Neither do I," she whispered.

For a few seconds he didn't move...not an eyelid, not a muscle. He didn't even seem to breathe as he digested her words and tried to decide how to react. Finally, his willpower obviously stretched beyond all reason, he heaved a ragged sigh and took her into his arms.

This time his kiss wasn't shy or tentative. His mouth opened to possess her lips, moving, tasting, molding to hers. The tip of his tongue no longer teased . . . it penetrated, slipping inside to caress the roof of her mouth and dirty dance with her tongue, matching its warmth.

He spread his hands across her back, pulling her closer, pressing her breasts against his bare chest. His own response to the increased intimacy was immediate and intense, swelling into a hard, hot muscle that dug into her stomach. The impressive show of masculinity didn't make her shy away. Instead it sent her own blood racing wildly through her veins, settling with a heated throb deep inside her.

"Shelly . . . I . . . we . . . are you sure you know what you're doing?" he gasped, forcing out the words between long, hungry kisses.

"Yes, Jim," she answered breathlessly, her head spinning from the delicious assault on her senses. "I'm not a silly little schoolgirl or an inexperienced virgin. I know what I want . . . and I want you."

"Oh, darlin' . . ." He slid his hands downward until they cupped her rounded bottom, pressing her against him. Her arms circled his neck and as he slowly lifted her, her legs wrapped around his waist. Their lips eagerly clung together as he carried her into the bedroom.

As he backed her up to the edge of the bed, he let her slowly slide down his body until she sat on the maroon and navy comforter. Her lips never left his skin as she moved them along his neck, over his broad

chest and down the hard, rippled muscles of his
stomach. His breath sucked in audibly as her tongue
circled his belly button, then followed the open vee of
his jeans.

When she met the denim barrier, she pulled her head
away and looked up at his flushed face. Her fingers
lifted to the row of metal buttons still holding the
jeans. His eyes drifted closed and his head rolled back
as her fingers brushed over the bulge that strained
against the material. So hard and ready was he that she
had difficulty maneuvering the buttons out of their
holes.

The instant the task was completed, her hands slid
inside the tight jeans and eased them down over his
hips. His swollen desire sprang free and, as if he could
no longer remain passive, he stepped out of the jeans
and impatiently kicked them aside.

"Look what you've done to me," he told her, his
eyes glazed with desire.

"Pretty impressive," she responded with a flirtatious grin.

"You ain't seen nothing yet." He leaned over her
and again captured her lips. He repaid her teasing
kisses by taking his time to slowly undress her, caress-
ing, licking and tasting various parts of her body as
they were revealed. When she was completely naked,
he paused for a few, anxious seconds, gazing down at
her. "You're even more beautiful than I imagined,"
he whispered in a ragged, awed voice.

He moved over her and gently pushed her backward until she was lying flat on the bed. Nestling between her legs, he hesitated, but this time they both
knew there was no turning back. He was simply de-
laying the inevitable, stretching the moment as he

kissed her with so much passion that she felt she would lose all control before he could even enter her. When neither of them could last another second, he spent a moment with a small package to ensure her protection, then eased inside her. She wrapped her legs around him, moving with his rhythm, urging him on. Gradually he quickened the pace, pushing deeper and deeper until she moaned aloud at the sensations the oak-hard, yet velvet-soft friction was causing inside her. She could feel his heart pounding in his chest as he brushed against her rigid nipples, and she knew her own heart was beating at the same erratic rate.

The desire that had been building inside her, practically since the first moment they'd met, wound tighter and tighter until it exploded like skyrockets of sparkling lights against a black satin sky. Ripples of an ecstasy so intense that it was almost painful blasted through her. Her muscles tensed, holding on to wave after wave of sensation that spiraled through her, until she felt as if it had drained the last drop of energy from her.

Just as she felt herself settling back to earth, she heard a guttural cry rip from his throat and felt him thrust even more deeply inside. Even as his body shook with emotion, she felt his hot passion pulse inside her, over and over, until he finally collapsed.

For several long, surrealistic moments, they lay together, their bodies bathed in the perspiration of lovemaking, their breathing shallow and irregular. Shelly struggled, but couldn't seem to form a single coherent thought as her body wound back down to normal.

Normal? She knew nothing would ever be the same for her again. Sex with her husband had always been good, but it had never been like this.

And now, lying in Jim's arms, she felt safe and loved. He shifted so the bulk of his weight was off her, but his arms tightened, holding her close, cradling her tenderly. His breath was warm against the sensitive skin of her neck, and she could feel the caress of an occasional kiss.

"You're wonderful," he whispered, his voice lazy and relaxed.

"So are you." Her eyes drifted closed in total satisfaction.

"Do you have to go home tonight?" He lifted his head just enough so he could look into her eyes. "I'd really like you to stay."

"That's good, because I honestly don't think I could move, even if I wanted to."

He sighed and nuzzled his face into the tangled pillow of her hair. "I'm glad to hear you don't want to." Even though she couldn't see his face, she knew he was smiling. "I've never asked a woman to spend the night with me here... but I can't imagine anything worse than waking up tomorrow without you in my arms."

Her heart that had so recently returned to its normal pattern did another little flip-flop. He reached out and pulled the edge of the comforter over them. She cuddled closer, seeking the warmth and affection his body offered. As she drifted off to sleep, his words echoed in her head. She loved him, and although he hadn't actually said it, she felt sure he loved her, too. Tomorrow they should talk.

Tomorrow...

JIM SLOWLY ROLLED over, awakening Shelly from the soundest sleep she'd had in years. "Good morning, honey," she murmured, lifting her hand to push her hair back from her face.

"I'm sorry. I didn't mean to wake you," Jim said in a soft, sexy voice.

"What time is it, anyway?" She could see the sun shining brightly through the crack in the burgundy drapes covering the bedroom windows.

Jim raised himself up on one elbow and looked at the clock. "It's ten-thirty. Do you need to go?"

"No. Not for a while," she answered, then hesitated. Maybe that had been her cue to leave. "That is, unless you have something else . . ."

He leaned over until his gaze captured hers. There was no doubting his sincerity as he said, "Nothing is more important than you and me, Shelly. And there's nothing I want more than to make love to you again right this minute."

His large hand gently cupped her cheek, and he bent forward to add emphasis to his statement with a long, loving kiss. Even though she felt his body react immediately, pressing with increasing urgency against her, he pulled away.

"I'll be back in a few minutes, darlin'." Jim got up and stretched. He gave her a sexy wink and that crooked, drop-dead grin that sent her blood racing through her veins in anticipation, then walked slowly and unself-consciously naked into the bathroom.

Shelly snuggled back into the plumpness of her pillow, hoping he wouldn't be long. Her stomach growled, reminding her that she'd skipped dinner last night and apparently breakfast this morning. And yet, the hunger she felt for Jim was more powerful than the emptiness of her stomach. She had a feeling she could never get enough of him.

It had been a long time since she'd lounged in bed so late in the morning...and even longer still since she'd lounged in bed with a man. And Jim was certainly *all* man.

Suddenly the stillness was broken when the phone rang. Her first response was to answer it, but she reminded herself she was merely a visitor. Besides, what if it was another woman? She really couldn't bear hearing a female voice asking for Jim. Especially not right now.

It rang again, then once more. Shelly turned her head to glare at it, as if that would silence the noise and chase away whoever was on the other end. When it rang a fourth time, there was a click and Jim's voice came over the answering machine.

"This is Jim. Leave a message and I'll get back to you."

She hadn't considered the possibility of an answering machine. With a groan she rolled over and covered her head with his pillow to drown out the voice of the caller.

However, a definitely masculine tone penetrated her barrier and she relaxed. She didn't mean to eavesdrop, but it was really impossible not to, as the oddly familiar voice on the other end said, "Sonny. This is Harlan. Listen, you need to stop playing games on this Mexico thing. The company's going to suffer if you and Shelly drag this out too long. Besides, I'm tired of covering for you. I'm in the office today until about noon. Give me a call here. I don't know how much longer I can keep this from her. She shouldn't find out who you are when you're nose to nose across the conference table. She deserves the truth . . . now."

Chapter Nine

Shelly sat up abruptly. Sonny? As in Sam Mitchell's Sonny...the same Sonny she'd heard so much about but still hadn't met? Why had Harlan called him here?

Could it have been a wrong number? But Harlan seemed certain he'd reached the party he was intending to call. And he hadn't even hesitated when Jim had said his name at the beginning of the message.

Harlan? Even if he hadn't identified himself, she'd have recognized his voice. It was definitely the same Harlan who was the attorney for Texas Pacific. But why had he called Sonny at Jim's apartment?

She pulled the sheet and blanket closer around her as if to seek comfort and protection. She suddenly felt very naked and very confused. Was this Sonny's apartment? Could Sonny be the friend Jim had referred to? Or could Sonny and Jim be the same...?

Her head was spinning. She didn't even want to consider the possibilities.

Shelly got up and gathered her clothes from around the room where they'd fallen as Jim had undressed her the night before. At first she moved absently as she dressed, but as thoughts began tumbling around in her head, her movements became more hurried, even frantic.

Jim? Sonny? Sonny? Jim? Could they be...?

Little flashes of memories flickered through her head like scenes from a movie. She saw the unexpectedly large amount of money bound by a gold money clip at the Yellow Rose. Where would a drifter have gotten so much cash so quickly? And even if he could justify that, why had he used a money clip? Now that she thought about it, it was very much out of character for a cowboy.

She remembered his hands, large, experienced hands that had brought so much pleasure to her last night. But while they weren't femininely soft, they weren't as callous and rough as they would be if he'd truly been doing manual labor on a railroad for any length of time.

How could Jim have known the way back to the ranch and how long it would take on that day they'd been out riding? And for that matter, he'd known exactly where to find things in the kitchen.

And what about Max? He'd acted like Jim was an old, long-lost friend. It was easy for a person to hide the truth, but a dog could always be counted on for total honesty. Especially if that dog was being reunited with his master.

Sonny? Jim? Jim? Sonny? The names twisted together as all the pieces of the puzzle began falling into place.

Shelly pressed her hands against her hot cheeks. He'd said she was the first woman he'd asked to spend the night here. At the time it hadn't seemed an odd thing to say. But now, as she considered it in a new light, she realized that might have been an impressive statement, if indeed Jim was Sonny and he'd been living here for several years. On the other hand, it could have been a big lie. *Another* lie. After all, truth didn't seem to be one of Jim's strong points.

And what about last night? Oh, Lord . . . last night. Her flush deepened as an embarrassment so overwhelming that she felt faint washed over her. She'd practically thrown herself at him. What must he think of her?

How could she not have known who he was? All the signs were there for her to read, and yet she'd missed them all. What a fool she'd been. How he must be laughing about this little game he was playing.

But then, what was his game?

Was it just the sex? Did he expect to win some important business conflict? Get his share of his father's inheritance? Or cut her out completely? All she knew was that she didn't want to deal with him on any of those issues at this moment.

She looked around the room as if seeing it for the first time. Her curiosity drew her to the dresser where a framed photo was lying facedown. Feeling absolutely no shame at her nosiness, she picked it up. As she stared at it, her fingers went numb and she almost dropped the gilt-edged frame.

Two people, an older woman and a young man stood together in front of the ranch house at the D-Rail. She didn't recognize the woman, but somehow she guessed she was Sam's wife—and Sonny's mother. But there was no doubt who the man was. Even though he was several years younger, he was definitely Jim. Dressed in a cap and gown, he'd obviously just graduated from college. And from the proud smile on the woman's face, she was evidently his mother. Sonny's mother, Shelly repeated to herself.

With a clatter she replaced the photo, then picked up a used airline ticket stub for a round-trip flight from San Antonio to Mexico City dated two weeks ago. And the name at the top was Jim Mitchell.

Jim Mitchell! The sound of running water in the bathroom reminded her that he could walk back into the bedroom at any moment. As chaotic as her thoughts were, the one thing that was perfectly clear was that she had to get out of this room, this apartment—immediately.

Shelly stepped into her shoes and didn't even stop to tie them as she headed for the bedroom door. But she'd taken only a few steps when Jim exited the bathroom, a large bath towel draped low around his waist.

"Where're you going?" he asked with obvious surprise. "I thought we'd go out for breakfast—" He flashed his devastating grin suggestively. "*After* we tell each other good morning properly."

Shelly could barely force herself to look at him, as her anger rose to a level that she could no longer control. "Oh really, *Sonny.* And just what did you have in mind?"

He rubbed his hand over his smooth-shaven jaw. "I just thought I'd get rid of the stubble..." His words trailed off as it dawned on him what she'd said. "Sonny?" he repeated cautiously.

"Yes, Sonny. That's your name, isn't it?"

His expression grew increasingly uneasy.

"Uh...no. My name is Jim."

For a moment the weight on her heart lifted. Could she have jumped to the wrong conclusion? Could she be wrong about this whole identity mix-up? Was Jim really just Jim? But before she could react, he continued.

"No one except my family and some of my oldest friends still call me Sonny. It's a nickname I outgrew years ago, but haven't been able to shake."

"So you're not denying it?"

He sighed and shook his head. "No...I can't."

She felt the salty heat of tears sting her eyelids as she pressed them closed. It was a crushing admission. She wasn't certain how she was going to deal with this whole situation, but she knew she couldn't let him see her cry. With a great effort she swallowed her pain and replaced it with a renewed burst of anger. "How could you deceive me like that? How? I trusted you completely. I even slept with you...the only man other than my husband..." Shelly bit her lower lip to keep it from trembling.

"How did you find out? How long have you known?" Jim was stunned.

"Is that all you care about? When were you going to tell me you were Sam's son? Or were you going to let it be a surprise when we came face-to-face at the board meeting tomorrow?" When he didn't answer immediately, she decided she couldn't stand to be in the same room with him for another moment and started for the door.

But he blocked her path by stepping in front of her. "I'd like to explain what happened. Please." Jim peered into her eyes, trying to appeal to her with a sincere look that had probably worked on countless women before her. "It isn't how it seems," Jim pleaded one more time.

"Oh yeah? Just how would it seem to you, Sonny? Or should I still call you Jim? I guess I don't really qualify as an old friend or a member of the family," Shelly said sarcastically. "What on earth could you possibly say at this point?" She tossed her head, sending her long, tangled hair back over her shoulder as she lifted her chin and glared at him, her heart breaking as she stood there. "You disgust me." Her anger wavered and she had to clench her teeth to keep her chin from quivering. "I disgust myself," she added, her voice barely above a whisper.

"I didn't mean for this to happen, Shelly."

"Which part? The sex? The lies? Or playing with my daughter's trust. Which part?" she repeated, then whirled around and walked to the window that looked out on the lake. She wrapped her arms across her chest in a protective gesture, wishing she would wake up from this nightmare and be safely in her bedroom at the ranch.

She didn't hear him approach, but she could smell the fresh, spicy fragrance of his after-shave and feel the heat of his body as he stepped closer and stopped behind her. Reluctantly she turned around. "Why did you do it? Sam's inheritance? Is that what this is all about?"

Jim looked at her for a moment, as Shelly waited expectantly for his response. His failure to answer was more eloquent than any words he could have said.

"Just as I thought. It *is* the inheritance," Shelly concluded with a disappointed nod. She'd still been holding on to one last hope that he had some sort of noble or even excusable reason, but he didn't make any attempt to keep the farce going.

"It *was* in the beginning," he admitted with an apologetic grimace. "I despised you for what my father had done. I thought you'd tricked him or that he'd lost his mind. But not anymore." Jim continued to study her face in the morning light as if searching for some sign that she believed his statements.

"In the beginning, huh?"

"Yeah. After I got to know you, I began to fall in love with you and everything changed."

She closed her eyes and let her head fall back. With a mirthless laugh, she retorted, "Love? What about all that business talk on the treaties and expansion into Mexico? Your idea of foreplay, I suppose?"

Jim's eyes shifted back and forth as he searched for a suitable response.

"You'd do or say anything to get your hands on your father's inheritance. It's the art of the deal, isn't it? A little sacrifice here...a little compromise there...sleep with whoever it takes to get what you want." The fury had returned to her in full force as she pierced him with an accusing glare. "You know, at first I felt guilty because he'd left it to me and cut you out. But the more I get to know you, the more I understand why he did it. You didn't even care enough to make it home for his funeral."

All the color drained from his face. "I tried. I even chartered a plane, when I couldn't get a commercial flight back quickly. But it had engine problems and we had to land about a hundred miles south of Del Rio. I hitched a ride to the border, rented a car and drove home. But I wasn't in time."

"I wish I could believe you. I hope, for Sam's sake, you're telling the truth, but I doubt you know the meaning of the word." She brushed past him, but she heard him following as she headed toward the front door, picking up her purse and her jacket on the way. "We have nothing else to discuss, Sonny, except across a boardroom table." Shelly opened the door, then glanced back. Even in the heat of anger, her heart twisted at the sight of him standing in the middle of the living room, his hair falling across his face and drops of water from his shower still clinging to his magnificent body.

But she managed to find strength from some deep, inner well of pride and self-respect. "I doubt that you'd bother to try since your plan obviously didn't work, but don't ever call me again. It's over." Her hand tightened on the knob as she started to pull the door shut. She paused again and added, "As for the TPRR, I've been screwed one too many times by you already. So if you think that I'm going to go along with any of your Mexico plans, you're dead wrong."

As she slammed the door behind her, the tears started to fall.

THE BRONCO SKIDDED to a stop in front of the ranch house. Shelly got out and stumbled over the steps as she ran to the front door, unlocked it and yanked it open. She walked into the den and collapsed on the padded leather chair behind the desk.

Staring at the large empty room, she imagined all that must have gone on in here while Sam was alive. Had he conducted high-powered meetings at this desk? Had he spent hours poring over schedules and financial reports and records of locomotive failures? Had Jim, when he was a baby, played on the floor at his father's feet?

She wished she could have just one more talk with Sam. There was so much she longed to ask him, so many answers she wanted and needed, so many loose ends that seemed to be hopelessly tangled.

"Oh, Sam... Sam," she whispered with a sigh. "What would you want me to do? Why did you think I could handle all this? I've never—"

But she didn't allow herself to finish the thought. Of course she'd never been in this position before with so much responsibility for so many people. However, that didn't mean she couldn't handle it. So far, life had thrown her many curves, but she'd always risen to the challenge and not only survived, but succeeded. What she lacked in industrial experience, could more than be made up for by her intelligence and the fact that she honestly cared about the effects of her decisions on other people. Besides, Sam had had faith in her, and she refused to let him down. She had things to prove... and people to prove them to.

She pushed the speakerphone button and dialed Harlan's office.

"Harlan here" came the slow drawl of his robust Texas accent.

"Harlan, this is Shelly. I need to talk to you about Sonny."

"Sonny? I was just trying to talk to him today about this Mexico deal. I—"

"Yeah, I know," she interrupted.

"What do you mean, you know?" Harlan asked, his tone cautious.

"I was at his apartment when you called and left a message earlier this morning."

A few minutes of silence stretched hollowly as Shelly waited for his reaction. Then, in a measured and deliberate tone, Harlan responded, "I tried to tell him to give it up. I know he was shocked by Sam's will..." Harlan paused, obviously trying to create a tense silence that would entice a response from Shelly.

Shelly had been married to an up-and-coming attorney, and she recognized it as an old lawyer's ploy. She remained quiet, keeping her thoughts and feelings to herself, prepared to outwait Harlan.

"Maybe we should talk about this tomorrow at the office?" Harlan finally asked.

"No. I want to know what's going on, and I want to know now," Shelly insisted. She wasn't going to let another day pass without finding out where she stood and who was with her or against her—and why.

"Where do you want me to start?" Harlan's tone changed, moving from reservation to open encouragement. Obviously he was as tired of the games as she was.

"For openers," demanded Shelly, "why was Jim coming on to me?"

"He thought you'd gotten Sam to change his will by manipulating him with your feminine charms and that you were completely unqualified to run TPRR. He was trying to find grounds to prove his father wasn't in command of his faculties or had been conned into changing his will to give you everything. I tried to talk Sonny out of it, but, apparently, he did it, anyway."

Shelly sensed there was something more. "What else? Come on, Harlan, tell me all of it."

The lawyer sighed reluctantly, but continued, "He was going to try to prove that you were a...uh..." He cleared his throat uneasily. "A hustler... a gold digger... a woman who'd taken advantage of Sam's advancing age and vulnerability."

Shelly gasped and could feel the redness return to her cheeks. She'd certainly played into Jim's hands last night, acting like a wanton woman and throwing herself into his bed.

"Why didn't you tell me?" she cried. "I trusted you."

"I didn't tell you because of my allegiance to Sam and his family. I know that's not really a good excuse, but maybe you can understand my position. You were a new and unknown factor, and I thought it would be best if I gave you time to see how things worked out. Besides, I figured Sonny would get this out of his system, and it'd be over before any damage could be done. No one the wiser, right?"

"No one the wiser, huh? Well, this leaves me in a pretty awkward position, doesn't it? I don't know who I can trust anymore. I could fire you right now, but I won't."

Obviously relieved, Harlan tried to assure Shelly of his loyalty. "I was trying to do what was best for the TPRR, that's all. I didn't take sides on the issue of Sam's will."

"What about the Mexico expansion? Where do you stand on that?" she asked.

"I can take it or leave it. There are advantages and disadvantages for TPRR, but I don't have a crystal ball to look into the future and see which is the best choice."

"None of us do," she commented wryly, "but a decision has to be made."

"And soon," Harlan added. "And Sonny hates to lose. He's lost the company, the ranch and now, you. He's not going to take losing the Mexico expansion project lying down. And he can be a formidable opponent.''

Shelly thought for a moment. ''Formidable or not, I'm sticking to my guns on this. Ol' Sonny will just have to get used to it, because he's going to lose another one.''

''HI, MAMA, I'm home,'' yelled Emily as she walked through the front door. ''Where are you?''

''I'm in here, honey,'' Shelly called from the kitchen where she stood, staring into the pantry.

Emily rushed in and gave her mother a hug and a kiss. ''I missed you last night. I called, but you must have gone to a movie or something.''

Shelly chose to ignore the last comment and said, ''I missed you, too. How was your sleepover?''

''Oh, we had a lot of fun. We called boys until one o'clock and then made pizza.''

''Boys? Uh...sounds wonderful. What would you like for dinner tonight?''

''Honestly? I'm sick of pizza and spaghetti. Can we have hamburgers or something?''

''Fine. Would you go get the meat out of the freezer for me?''

''Sure, Mama.'' Emily skipped out of the room and returned quickly with the frozen meat. ''Are you going to see Jim tonight? Can we all do something together?''

Shelly thought for a moment about what she would tell Emily. The girl had grown very fond of Jim and looked forward to doing things with him. But since he was out of her personal life forever, she might as well be honest. ''Emily, I'm not going to see Jim anymore.''

"Why not?" Emily asked. "You guys were neat together."

Shelly turned, focusing on the preparation of their meal so her daughter wouldn't notice her tears. "Let's just say he's not the man I thought he was."

Chapter Ten

"Glad you're here, Harlan," said Shelly, as she got up from behind the desk in her office. "We've got a lot to talk about."

"I know you're still annoyed with me, Shelly. I knew he was desperate, but I had no idea what he was doing," Harlan stated, as he sat in the chair across the desk from her. "And I certainly didn't know he was dating you."

"Would you have said anything had you known?"

"I don't know," he responded thoughtfully. "But you've got to believe me when I tell you my loyalty was to Sam and this company. I only want what's best."

Shelly stared at Harlan for a moment, then nodded. "Okay, let's get to work." Shelly sat and shuffled the papers she'd been reviewing off to one side, replacing them with a legal pad.

"First," Harlan began, "we need to discuss when we'll be able to make a final decision on the expansion. I don't think you have the votes today to keep it from passing...if that's what you want to do. You need to give the members a meeting or two to get to know who you are and learn to trust your judgment."

"What would happen if I pushed the vote today?"

"If you're wrong and you lose, then the line to Mexico goes in."

"And if I wait?" asked Shelly, raising her eyebrows expectantly.

"If you wait and can convince a few of the others to get off the fence and see it your way, you'll quash the whole idea."

She considered Harlan's advice for a moment. "And if I win? Then what? What happens to Jim?" Shelly was annoyed to hear the inflection of concern in her voice. After all he'd done, she shouldn't care one way or the other about Jim. And yet ...

"He'll have lost all influence with his father's company. He'd be well advised to sell out and move on. Texans, and especially railroaders, don't think much of a loser."

"Loser? Is that what people will think? Really?" Shelly hadn't thought about consequences beyond how the decision would affect the company.

"That's right." Harlan opened his notebook and began scanning the pages he'd brought with him.

Shelly knew she'd have to think that angle over more carefully, although she knew it wouldn't be wise to let Jim's personal consequences influence her in any way. "What else?"

"We need to respond to the request we have had to return some of our abandoned rights-of-way to Brazoria County."

"We're not using those tracks?"

"Actually the tracks were pulled up a couple of years ago for scrap. All that remains are the ties and the contaminated ballast and soil. They're willing to give us a token $10,000 for it. Or we could donate it and get a tax write-off."

"What is ballast and soil? What do you mean contaminated?" Shelly sat up straighter in the chair. This was not at all what she'd expected to deal with when she'd taken over the company. She'd thought it was all locomotives, cabooses and contracts, not environmental issues. "How did it get contaminated in the first place?"

"Through the years the chemicals we hauled over all our lines have leaked and spilled. Until now nobody cared." Harlan explained the Federal law. "If we sell or donate the land, we're liable for the expense of the cleanup. You have about an even split on the committee, so how you handle it will dictate how it goes."

"I suppose Jim is on the side to keep the land," Shelly commented.

"You got it. He figures the land is more valuable under our ownership than in the hands of the county. Especially if we have to pay for it to be cleaned up."

"Who owned the rail cars that hauled those chemicals over our lines?"

"Most of the chemical companies that have refineries on the Gulf Coast. Why do you ask?"

"Oh, something Sam mentioned to me one time about taking responsibility for your own actions. So, since their cars leaked their chemicals on our land, why should we pay to have it cleaned up?"

Harlan sat for a moment and looked curiously at Shelly. "Good point, Ms. Lowell. Good point."

BY THE TIME Shelly and Harlan entered the meeting room, all the participants had been seated and waiting for several minutes. It was an inauspicious beginning.

As Harlan held the door open and Shelly walked in, all eyes were focused on her. *Stay calm,* she admonished herself, then paused for a moment scanning the attendees around the table. Finally her gaze settled on Jim.

He returned her look boldly, even daring to give her a hint of that crooked grin. Shelly gave him the same polite, professional smile she'd given all the others, then moved away. She walked slowly to the far end of the room where her seat was located at the head of the table. Sam sure had known how to play the power position.

She set her notebook and handouts for the meeting on the table and sat down. "Gentlemen. I've asked Harlan to run today's meeting until I'm more familiar with the procedure. I hope to get together with each of you individually within the next few days." Glancing around the room, she swallowed the nervous lump that threatened to block her throat and looked at Harlan. "Please proceed, Mr. Dickerson."

"Thank you, Ms. Lowell. We have two items on the agenda this week. One is to decide when we will give a final written response to the Mexican government proposal for our rail line expansion into Mexico. The second agenda item concerns our donation of the fifteen miles of the Mustang Bayou branch line to Brazoria County. I suggest we take the branch line donation first." Harlan looked around to verify that all were in agreement. Hearing no objections he went on, "I'm sure you've all read the proposal. Discussion?"

Jim spoke up. "Just how much will it cost us to clean up those fifteen miles?"

"Preliminary estimates range between $175,000 and $300,000," Charles Spurrier explained. "It depends on how deep they have to dig and the exact nature of the contaminants."

"I say the decision's clear." Jim rose from his seat at the table and leaned forward, bracing himself with his hands spread on the polished oak surface as he pointedly met everyone's gaze except Shelly's. "There are no choices in the matter. We can't afford to go around cleaning up all the land that's under our tracks. I say we vote no and get on with the next item." Jim straightened and turned the full effect of his silvery blue eyes on her. "What do you think, Ms. Lowell? Have any better ideas?"

Actually she'd been thinking how unbelievably handsome he looked in his charcoal gray suit. The vivid whiteness of his shirt made him look more tanned and healthy than ever before. His dark hair was neatly combed and was almost black in the artificial light. He'd looked wonderful dressed in cowboy gear and now was impressive as an executive. The only time he'd looked better was that night as he stood next to her while she sat on the bed and undressed him....

But Shelly knew this was no time to let her mind wander to places it had no business being. With a mental shake, she knew if she didn't meet this first challenge, she would lose all credibility with her executives. She pushed her chair back from the table. Slowly she rose and stood without speaking until Jim sat down. When she had everyone's attention, she began to speak in a deceptively calm voice.

"Excellent point, *Sonny*," she said somewhat sarcastically. "I've been looking into the situation a little further and think there is an acceptable alternative."

She picked up the stack of handouts that she and Harlan had hurriedly compiled, listing names and amounts offered by various companies. She passed the stack to the man on her left, who took one and passed them on. "At my request, Harlan contacted the chemical customers whose cars we pulled along that fifteen-mile stretch all those years." Turning toward Jim, she continued, "They all agreed to help pay for the cleanup."

"At what price?" demanded Jim. "They aren't going to pay their fair share of two or three hundred thousand dollars without canceling their contracts with us. We need their business." Jim looked around at the others as if gauging their reactions.

"True. But that isn't exactly my plan. How much is that land worth on the open market?"

"My guess would be around $250,000. Maybe more."

"Then I suggest," Shelly said, "we sell the land to our customers and allow them to share in the tax deduction associated with giving the land back to the county. That way, we all get good press out of this and at no cost to us." Shelly sat down and pulled her chair up to the table. The executives were studying their handouts, murmuring to those around them and nodding their heads, so she felt confident they saw the advantage to her proposal. "So, Harlan, could we vote on this now?"

"Any further discussions?" Harlan asked, glancing around the room. "Hearing none. Those in favor of Shelly's proposal, signify by raising your hand." Harlan's gaze circled the table and everyone but Jim's hand was raised. Slowly his, too, lifted to join the others. "All those opposed to Shelly's proposal, raise your hand," Harlan asked for the record, noting there were none.

"I guess that settles it. Ms. Lowell, if I have your permission, I'll begin work on the details with the chemical companies right away."

"Certainly, Harlan," Shelly responded, resisting the urge to give Jim a smug smile. This was business, and she shouldn't allow her personal feelings to reduce her to his level.

"The next item on the agenda is," Harlan said, again leading the meeting, "to make a decision as to when we will respond to the Mexican Government on their request that we extend rail service across the border."

Recognizing that she had the upper hand, Shelly was eager to present her ideas regarding the Mexico question. But she remembered what Harlan had told her about possible results if she tried to push for a decision today. "Considering the significance of this issue, I move we table this until next week."

"I second the motion," responded Harlan. "It'll give us time to study the final numbers. Jim has prepared a report which gives all the details we should need." Harlan motioned for Jim to pass out the documents.

"I think this will answer all your questions," Jim stated. "I see no reason not to move ahead with this plan immediately. We're losing money every day we delay laying that first rail. We need to act quickly and sign an agreement with Mexico before someone else beats us to it." Jim spoke with renewed confidence as

the other executives began leafing through his report
with interest.

"And I think we all need time to thoroughly read
this very well-prepared report so we can make an ed-
ucated decision," Shelly commented, then smiled at
the other men at the table. "Gentlemen, I'm asking
your indulgence, but I'm uncomfortable acting on
something of this magnitude without knowing all I can
about the proposal."

"I think that's only fair," Charles Spurrier agreed.

"Yes, so do I," another man said, and they all, with
the exception of Jim, nodded their approval.

"Any further discussions?" asked Harlan. "Hearing none, we'll postpone the vote on the Mexican expansion until next week. This meeting is adjourned."

Shelly could practically feel the heat of Jim's anger
as she mingled with the other executives. She knew
she'd have to spend long hours going over his report
with a fine-tooth comb. She'd be prepared for the
meeting next week if it killed her.

IT HADN'T BEEN a good day. Hell, Jim thought, as he
massaged the knotted muscles at the back of his neck,
it hadn't been a good month.

He looked at the pile of papers on his desk. Charts,
graphs and financial analyses were spread across the
oak surface—documents that proved, at least to him,
that the Mexico expansion was an opportunity TPRR
couldn't afford to miss. If only he could make that
hard-headed woman in his father's office listen.

But he was afraid he'd cut off all hope of amicable
communications between Shelly and himself. When
he'd hatched his plan, he'd certainly never imagined
this result. Of course, he hadn't anticipated falling in

love with his adversary...but it had happened. She wouldn't listen to that, either.

She'd proven to be more intelligent and infinitely more appealing than he'd expected. Oh, sure, he'd assumed the woman who'd convinced his father to change his will would be attractive. He'd also predicted she'd be sly, conniving and subtly manipulative. Even as he grew closer to Shelly, gradually breaking through her protective layers until he'd reached the vulnerable, passionate woman underneath, he'd analyzed her every move carefully, searching for the con artist he'd anticipated.

But Shelly was real. She was probably the most genuinely sincere person he'd ever met. It hadn't fit his image, and he certainly hadn't known how to deal with the discovery. He'd known all along that sooner or later she'd find out about his deceit. What he hadn't counted on was that he would care what she thought— or care that she would be hurt.

The evening she'd come to his apartment, he'd been sitting on the couch, trying to think of a way to tell her the truth, the whole truth, without chasing her away. When she'd arrived and things had progressed so quickly to his bedroom, all thoughts but making love to her had been pushed aside.

That, in itself, was a first for him. He'd never been with a woman that his active mind hadn't been wandering off on other subjects such as what time his plane left the next day or whether he'd remembered to pack his swim trunks. Never had a woman been able to dominate his thoughts, no matter what he was doing. Somehow Shelly was different. She'd managed to fill his mind, excite his body and touch his heart.

Unfortunately she'd discovered his masquerade before he'd had a chance to soften the blow. By the time he'd had an opportunity to speak, she'd already worked herself into a frenzy.

Jim leaned back in his chair and propped his feet up on his credenza. He knew that wasn't a fair description. Of course she was upset. But more than that, he knew she felt betrayed and hurt. He'd learned long ago that one of the most important elements of any successful relationship, whether it was business or personal, was trust. And, his not-so-wise plan had destroyed that with Shelly. The possibility existed that he would never be able to win that trust back. He could try, but until he did convince her, he knew she wouldn't believe anything he had to say...especially that he might be in love with her.

"Oh, what a tangled web we weave..." he muttered, remembering one of his mother's favorite sayings.

And it wasn't helping his case that he and Shelly were on opposite sides of almost every issue that faced TPRR. She'd surprised him today, proving to be a formidable and persuasive opponent. Things promised to get even more adversarial during the next week. It could very likely be a death knell to any hope that they'd be able to work through their personal differences.

He heaved a long sigh. It was ironic, he thought, that the person who could have been the woman of his dreams would turn out to be the woman who would take them all away.

"Uh...Jim...do you need me for anything else?"

Jim looked up at his secretary, who was standing in the doorway of his office. A glance at the clock on his desk told him it was after six. "No, Virginia, you can go home. I'll be leaving as soon as I put all this stuff back in the file."

The matronly woman hesitated, her lips curved into a hint of a smile. "It's good to have you back."

"Thanks."

She shut the door behind her, and Jim quickly gathered up the documents and replaced them in a thick file folder in the lower drawer of his desk. He could take it home tonight, but he knew he wouldn't be able to concentrate on it. Besides, he knew the report backward and forward. All he could do was try to convince the other executives into voting his way at the next meeting. If he couldn't win her over, at least he didn't have to watch the railroad wither and die. And he was truly convinced that would be its fate if this Mexican deal was not finalized soon.

He put on his trench coat and locked his office door. The sun was already behind the hills, and the last light of the long day was streaking across the sky in orange and gold waves as he made his way out of the building and to his car. He didn't notice Shelly until they practically bumped into each other in the almost deserted parking lot. She was fumbling through her key ring, searching for the door key to the Bronco, when she looked up and saw him.

There was a mixture of fear, anger and confusion in her dark, expressive eyes. He sensed she didn't know whether to acknowledge his presence or to merely get away as quickly as possible.

Jim knew exactly what he wanted to do. He wanted to pull her into his arms and hold her against him. He wanted to kiss her and tell her it had all been a mistake. He wanted to chase away her suspicions and begin the delicate task of reestablishing the trust and affection he'd felt before she knew he was Sonny.

"Hi." He was surprised by the butterflies that fluttered in his stomach, as if he was a schoolboy talking to a girl in the hallway between classes.

"Hello," she responded cautiously.

"I wanted to compliment you on your suggestion about the contamination cleanup this morning." He grinned, hoping he could somehow coax her lovely lips into an answering smile. "Wish I'd thought of it."

But her mouth remained grim as she shifted her heavy briefcase to her other hand. "Thanks. Now if you'll excuse me—"

"Of course, the busy tycoon on her third week on the job. I should have known."

"Actually, it's the busy tycoon on her way home to spend some time with her daughter."

"How is Emily?" he asked. He hadn't been around many children, but he'd enjoyed the time he'd spent with Shelly and her daughter.

However, Shelly showed her disbelief that his interest might be sincere with an unladylike snort. "You really don't have to keep pretending, you know."

He knew he could protest and proclaim his real feelings until he was blue in the face, but he'd be wasting his breath. Shelly simply wasn't willing or able at this time to believe anything he said. But he couldn't help but give it one last shot. "Look, why don't we go somewhere for dinner and talk about us?"

Shelly gave him a disdainful look and pivoted away from him. She inserted her key into the lock and, without looking back at him, stated, "There is no *us*. As far as I'm concerned, Jim Connors is dead. And I don't think it's wise, considering the circumstances, that you and I discuss anything other than business."

Jim stared at her stiffened back as she opened the door. She struggled with her tight suit skirt, trying to take that first big step up into the Bronco without sacrificing a shred of her steely poise. Was it anger? Was it vanity? Was it pride? Or was it uneasiness at being caught in her own game?

As he watched her, his eyes narrowed. She was blowing this all out of proportion. Here he was, trying to apologize, and she wouldn't even meet his eyes. It was almost as if she was the one feeling guilty.

Guilty about what? Had he been right all along? Had her fling with "Jim" just been an unexpected diversion? But now that she knew who he was, she couldn't face him, because she knew she'd cheated him out of his inheritance?

"You got exactly what you wanted, didn't you?" he asked, his voice dangerously low and strained.

"What are you talking about?" Shelly settled on the truck's seat and paused in her attempt to pull the hem of her skirt down to cover her thighs.

"My father never knew what hit him." Jim raked his fingers through his hair and gave a humorless chuckle. "Hell, your charms worked on me, too, and I went into it with my eyes wide open. Lady...and I use that term loosely...you are even better than I gave you credit for."

Shelly's hands stilled and all the color drained out of her face. "I never—"

"Probably not, but you would have if my dad had lived long enough. You'd have done anything to provide a home for yourself and your daughter. *Anything.*"

She was silent for a long moment, then she lifted her chin. "Yes, I wanted to take care of my daughter, but I'd *never* stoop so low as to take advantage of a lonely old man."

"I'm sure you made his last days *much* more enjoyable." Jim made no attempt to hide his disgust.

But Shelly snapped back at him. "You should talk, *Sonny.* Your father wouldn't have been so lonely if you'd loved him just a little bit. If you'd been there for him, he wouldn't have had to spend his nights eating stale pie in a two-bit café with strangers."

"You don't give up, do you? You don't know anything about my relationship with my father. It was…" He struggled to find the right words, as an avalanche of emotions welled inside him. "Whatever it was, it had nothing to do with you. Well, I'll fight you for my inheritance. You've had your fifteen minutes of fame, but don't unpack your bags, because you won't be here long. You may have blinded my father, but I refuse to let you ruin this company." Jim jerked open his car door, then added a final challenge. "You won't win so easily next week. You can bank on that!"

If he'd been expecting tears or anger or fear, he was disappointed. Instead, a confident smile curved across her full lips. "Do you want to bet on that?" she asked.

"Yeah—name it."

Her smile widened, and she nodded toward his car. "Is this your Vette? So the truck was all part of the disguise, huh?"

Jim shrugged, unwilling to show any hint of remorse for his actions.

"Okay, then put your car where your mouth is."

"And what are you putting up?"

"Everything," she answered solemnly. She shut her door and rolled down her window just far enough so he could hear her add, "We both know that whoever wins that showdown next week will win it all, anyway."

He gave her a stiff nod of acceptance. "Then may the best man win," he said sarcastically.

"Thanks . . . I will."

With a last cocky grin, she started the engine, backed out of the space and left him in a cloud of dust.

Chapter Eleven

"Mr. Coggins and Mr. Tracy are on the phone." Nancy announced through the intercom.

Shelly got up from her seat on the large leather sofa in her office where she'd been reading Jim's report and walked to her desk. Quickly she flipped through Sam's telephone directory, but didn't locate either name. "Did they say who they were with?"

"No, but I'll ask."

Shelly sat in her chair behind the desk and watched the light stop blinking as Nancy went back on the line to inquire as to the nature of this call. When the light began blinking, Nancy again spoke through the intercom.

"They're with Intercontinental Finance Services. I don't recognize their names, but they said they're old friends of Sam and financial backers of the railroad."

"I'll talk with them. Thanks." Shelly punched the blinking light and transferred the call to the speakerphone. "This is Shelly Lowell. How can I help you?" she asked in her best business voice.

"Ms. Lowell, I'm Sandy Coggins in Chicago, and I have Jack Tracy from our San Francisco office on the phone, also."

She was a little intimidated that she had no clue who these men were or how important they were to the company, so she allowed them to continue without comment.

"As you are aware, we own fifteen percent of the stock in the Texas Pacific Railroad, and we wanted to check out some rumors we've heard since you assumed the chairmanship of the company. I'm sure you can understand our concern."

"This is Jack Tracy, Mrs. Lowell, and I'll get right to the point. Is TPRR going to move into the Mexican market now or rebuild their existing lines? The decision you make may result in a significant difference as to the financial outlook of the company. Even more serious is the appearance that the leadership of the TPRR is in such confusion and conflict that it can't get out of its own way."

"The Mexican expansion is the number-one item on the agenda at our executive committee meeting next Monday," stated Shelly in a voice that was much more confident than she felt. In fact, this whole week, ever since her confrontation with Jim in the parking lot, she'd been the picture of confidence on the outside, successfully hiding the turmoil of indecision inside.

"Every day that goes by causes increased concern in the financial community. Time-delays increase the cost of any refinancing we're doing. It could even spell the ruin of the TPRR, Ms. Lowell. As its chairman, you must get this battle for control under control." Jack's voice had grown increasingly louder and harsher in tone.

"I appreciate your concern, gentlemen. As a matter of fact, I was studying the reports on the expansion before you called. We fully agree on the importance of this matter, and, although it may seem otherwise, we are working together for the future of TPRR," Shelly said passionately. "Jim and I may disagree on the means, but we're both committed to the success of this company."

Jack must have recognized her sincerity because his voice was calmer as he said, "Then we can trust you'll notify us as soon as a decision is reached? And we can pass on to our investors that TPRR's internal problems are in the process of being resolved?"

"Yes, gentlemen, I can guarantee that by early next week, the leadership, as well as the direction of TPRR will be clearly defined. I'm sure you'll work with us no matter which path is chosen." Even as she did her best to reassure these two men, she knew they were absolutely right. She must take the lead on a quick, distinct resolution or risk the financial integrity of Sam's company. "Thank you for bringing this to my attention." Shelly's voice tapered off in hopes of ending the conversation at this point.

"We hope you'll be successful. We don't envy you having to deal with Jim. From all Sam has said about him, he must be a real loose cannon," Sandy commented. "Goodbye, Ms. Lowell."

"We look forward to working with you in the future," Jack added.

"Thank you. Goodbye, gentlemen." With a deep breath of relief, Shelly pressed the disconnect button on the speakerphone and leaned back in her chair. She knew she needed to do something...but what? This job had grown in complexity by leaps and bounds, and Jim was no help. In fact, he was doing everything in his power to make her task more difficult. Obviously he'd love to see her fail just to prove his father had made a huge mistake. Well, Sam hadn't made a mistake, and she would prove it.

She pushed herself out of the chair and returned to the couch where she picked up Jim's report. She'd already read it through once and was now going back over it with a highlighter while jotting notes on a legal pad. He'd presented some compelling arguments for the Mexican expansion. Shelly was trying very hard to view the document through Sam's eyes to see why he'd objected so strenuously to the project. There had to be something she was missing, some important piece that Jim had intentionally understated or misrepresented.

Or maybe he was just setting her up, lulling her into not looking too deeply so he could spring some sort of surprise on her next Monday. Well, she'd be the one to spring the surprise. She would know everything there was to know about the expansion so she'd be ready for anything. She might have gone into this business knowing nothing about it, but she wouldn't end her possibly very brief career as a railroad executive without a fight.

JIM SAT IN HIS OFFICE with the door closed. It was near the end of the day, and he didn't want to deal with the affairs of the railroad anymore today. He was tired of speculating on the upcoming business battles with Shelly. In fact, he wished he could somehow push her completely out of his thoughts. Just when he would work himself into righteous anger, he would remember the way her eyes sparkled when she laughed or how her hair had looked flowing across the pillow after they'd made love.

That night had ruined it for him. He couldn't even remember the other women he'd made love to, because none had ever mattered for more than a few hours. But it had been different with Shelly.

In spite of all he knew about her...her marriage and her child...and all he suspected about her...her affair whether consummated or not with his father, there was an innocence about her that had touched his very soul. Everything had been fresh and new with her as if he was experiencing it all for the first time.

She'd been through some rough times, and yet she'd made the best of her situation until the stroke of luck in the form of his father had entered her life and given her a new beginning. But even with more wealth and power than she could have ever imagined having, she hadn't gone wild.

He'd truly never thought she would take her job at the TPRR so seriously. He'd tried everything, from intimidation to trying to outsmart her, but she'd stuck in there. From all the reports he'd heard, she was spending long hours researching the expansion as well as reviewing the personnel files and trying to meet every employee personally. That was more than Jim had done. For that matter, he doubted even his father had made such an effort after the company grew so large.

She'd consistently made it clear that she would never acknowledge any personal relationship with him, so he'd finally accepted that it was over. Perhaps if they weren't also forced into working together, things could be settled between them. But with his deception and his father's will standing between them as a constant reminder of their situation, he couldn't see how such difficult obstacles could be overcome.

But his brief relationship with her had had an unexpected side effect that was causing him long hours of self-analysis. Looking back on his life and past relationships, he wasn't very proud of himself. By trying to escape from the domination of his father, he'd gone a little overboard in proving his independence. Ironically, he'd treated everyone just as his father had treated him, as if by cutting down other people, he would be making himself look better. The truth was he'd used whoever he needed at the moment with no thought for their feelings or welfare. Even Shelly.

It was a very sobering realization. He wished he could blame it all on his father, but he had to be man enough to accept the responsibility of his actions. He'd simply chosen a poor way to deal with his own insecurities. But it wasn't too late to find new and more acceptable solutions to his problems.

Jim honestly didn't know why his father had never accepted him, once he'd become an adult. Maybe his father simply hadn't known how to show his affection, or perhaps he had expected too much of a young boy. He'd never been physically cruel, but he'd never been emotionally supportive, either. But that was his father's problem, and Jim couldn't let old grudges ruin his life.

The truth that Jim had come to realize was that it had not been his fault, and he couldn't go through life letting it destroy him. His father had been a saint to some people, but Jim had seen the other side. And he knew he could rise above that and be a better human being. Yet it would always hurt, and there would always be those questions that would now go unanswered forever.

He'd lost his father. He'd had the home and company he'd always expected to inherit disappear out from under him. He'd bungled any relationship he might have had with a wonderful woman because of his suspicions and paranoia. Now it was time Jim stopped fighting the windmills of his past and focused on his future.

His contemplation was interrupted by a knock on the door. "Yes?" he asked, then realized his door was closed and his secretary couldn't hear him. He pushed the intercom button and repeated the question.

Instead of answering, Virginia opened the door and stepped inside the office. "You have two gentlemen to see you." She indicated with a shrug of her shoulders that she had no idea who they were.

"Two?" He glanced down at his calendar and realized immediately who the two men were, even though they weren't noted on his appointment calendar. And neither had he mentioned them to his secretary, because they were part of his own personal quest to right the wrong his father's will had perpetrated. But he wanted to see them one at a time, so he could hear their reports separately. "Oh, right. Have Mr. Fitzgerald come in first. Stu can wait."

Virginia left and, in a moment, returned with a gentleman by her side. "Can I get anything for you, sir?" she asked.

The man shook his head.

"No, thanks," Jim told her, then waited until she'd closed the door behind her. "Have a seat, Joe." Jim motioned toward a chair across from his desk.

"I've completed my assignment," the detective began, taking a folder out of his briefcase and placing it on the desk in front of Jim.

He picked up the folder, but didn't open it. He didn't know if he really wanted to hear the results or not. It could mean the end to his hopes. Not only could he lose his company, but all hope of ever seeing Shelly again. "Well, what did you find out?"

"I believe we can make a case that your father was of unsound mind when he changed his will and left everything to that waitress."

Jim closed his eyes and exhaled a deep breath. Was that good news or bad? "What did you find out?"

"Your father had been under a doctor's care for the last three years."

"I didn't know," Jim murmured, truly surprised.

"Apparently no one did. And I don't think he wanted anyone to, either. He drove into Austin to visit a Dr. Gerald at least once a month, and more often toward the end."

"Was he a specialist of some sort?"

Joe hesitated for a moment as if reluctant to break the news so coldly. "He was an oncologist."

"My father had cancer?" Jim was shocked. There had never been any indication that his father had been sick a day in his life.

"I didn't have access to the files, but the doctor indicated Mr. Mitchell had an inoperable brain tumor. He was, if you'll pardon the expression, one of the lucky ones, because it was in a location that didn't cause him to lose *all* of his mental faculties. It was simply a matter of time until the tumor grew too large and cut off the blood supply to the brain, causing a quick and relatively painless death."

It took Jim a few minutes for the startling news to sink in. Of all the things he'd expected to hear, this was definitely the most surprising. He felt a sudden surge of relief that his father's strange behavior might have had a valid cause. It offered an explanation for the discrepancies in Sam's life, such as his loss of interest in the company and his refusal to consider growth and progress, as well as the rejection of his son. "But you said it didn't affect his mental capabilities?"

"No, I said he didn't lose *all* of them. What happened was something similar to the symptoms of Alzheimer's disease. While he could continue with his normal activities, his judgment and even his memory were failing. But he was a strong man and obviously able to hide it from everyone around him. Especially since, from all the sources I've talked to, Sam had withdrawn from his old friends and spent more time alone...or, apparently, with his new friend at the Spur."

"His new friend who didn't know how he used to be and couldn't ask uncomfortable questions," Jim mused. "Someone who would accept him just as he was."

"I suppose that could have been part of her appeal." Joe nodded. "I'll have to be honest with you and say that there is no indication whatsoever that Ms. Lowell ever met with your father outside that diner. If she did, either no one witnessed it or wants to talk about it."

Deep in his heart Jim had already accepted that probability, even though it had been easier for him to dislike Shelly if he was able to keep telling himself that she'd been physically involved with Sam.

"Of course, we could still make a case against her, implying that she enticed him, luring him into changing his will. It would be easy to show that they'd established a deep bond in a very short period of time. Her own background of a teenage pregnancy won't help her image. And..." Joe paused while he reached into his briefcase for another folder. "I found evidence that she shared an apartment with a man for several months back in Atlanta before she moved here."

Jim leaned back in his chair. This news surprised him almost as much as that of his father's illness. "Are you sure?"

"Positive. Of course, the man claims they were just friends, sharing expenses because she was trying to stretch her salary as far as possible. But no one was there with them, so it'd just be their word against whatever nasty thoughts the jury will probably have. And we'll do everything in our power to plant every possible sexual implication in their minds."

Jim shifted uncomfortably. He knew Shelly well enough to believe her ex-roommate's story. And, to be fair, even if she'd had an affair with the guy, it wasn't really any of his business and had no bearing on his father's will. But he could see the potential for turning the information to benefit his case.

"So, where do we go from here?" he asked Joe.

"I'll write up a deposition of my findings and have it notarized. We can subpoena Dr. Gerald's files and even Ms. Lowell's old roommate. All we have to do is show a pattern of unusual behavior by your father and show a possibility that Ms. Lowell could have taken advantage of his confusion and vulnerability, and we'll have an excellent chance of invalidating his last will." Joe stood and handed Jim the file on Shelly. "These copies are for you."

"Thanks. I'll be getting back to you shortly. I need to move on this as fast as possible," stated Jim as he got up and walked around his desk to show the private investigator out.

"Virginia? Send in my next appointment," Jim requested as he stood by the door to his office.

Jim's attorney extended his hand as he approached the office door. "Good to see you, Jim. I trust Joe filled you in on all the details."

"Come on in, Stu," Jim said as he stepped aside, allowing the other man to enter his office first. Stu had been Jim's personal attorney since he first reached legal age, and he was a trusted friend.

Jim picked up the two folders Joe had left and joined Stu on the couch. "Well, what do you think about this information?"

"You should be very pleased. Based on what your investigator found out, there is a strong legal precedence to have your father's will contested successfully. You will, of course, have to allow me some freedom to get the facts out on the table."

"Such as what?" Jim asked.

"First, with the evidence from that doctor in Austin we shouldn't have any trouble establishing that your father was not of sound mind when he changed his will to leave everything to Shelly. Of course, she'll have to be our key witness. Hostile, of course."

"Shelly? Why?"

Stu nodded. "Her account of your father's behavior at the end is crucial to our case. It seems no one knew him better in his final months," he stated matter-of-factly.

Jim was not pleased at the prospect of putting Shelly through that ordeal. For some reason he'd believed he would be able to prove his case without actually involving her, which was really a joke now that he thought about it. Of course she'd have to testify. But the realization that they would be actively and very publicly raking her reputation over the coals was alarming.

"But wouldn't that be a conflict of interest for her? I mean she'll have to say things that will jeopardize herself, won't she?"

"To be perfectly honest, Shelly's past and her situation at the time of her knowing Sam will make our case. It shouldn't be difficult to expose her as a gold digger who was able to prey on the confusion of a lonely old man."

Jim sat in silence as he thought about Stu's strategy. With a resigned sigh Jim said, "You know best. Do what you have to do. Thanks for coming over." Jim got up from the couch and walked with Stu to the door.

"Call me if you have any questions Jim. I'll get the paperwork started." Stu turned and departed without further discussion.

Jim glanced over at his secretary who was still sitting at her desk. "You can go home early today, Virginia, I'm about through myself."

"Thanks, Jim. I'll see you Monday," she said as she shut off her computer and picked up her purse. She glanced over at him with a worried expression. "You look upset. Is there anything I can do for you?"

Jim thought for a moment and then spoke softly. "Would I be wrong to contest my father's will?"

Virginia seemed surprised at his question. "Are you thinking of trying to do that?"

"I don't know what to do. I just don't know. Do I have the right to ruin two people's reputations...?" His voice tapered off to where he couldn't be heard.

"Two people?"

Jim looked up as if he was surprised that she was still there. "Oh, nothing. Have a nice weekend." He turned and headed back into his office.

Still she hesitated. "Uh...I know it's not any of my business, but are you and Ms. Lowell getting serious about each other?"

That comment brought his head jerking around. "Why would you ask that?"

"Word got around that you and she were dating. I know it's none of my business, but I think the two of you would make a terrific couple."

"Yeah. She's a very special person. But there's nothing going on between us."

Virginia persisted. "But you really do like her, don't you, Jim?"

His smile was wistful. "More than anyone knows...including her," he answered softly. "But it doesn't matter. She hates me now, and if I go through with my plans, she'll hate me even more." He sighed. "We never really had a chance."

Chapter Twelve

Shelly sat at her desk, her chair turned toward the large window through which the early-morning sunlight bathed her office. But now, in mid-afternoon, the railway yard below was covered in ever-lengthening shadows.

Jim's report lay open in her lap, but her eyes were focused outside, well past the arriving and departing locomotives, to the gently rolling hills beyond. Her mind was filled with facts and figures that had, instead of clearing up the issue, made it more complex. Considering Jim's presentation, how could she vote no? Considering Sam's opposition, how could she vote yes?

She took a sip of her tepid coffee and laid her head back as if in a deep meditation...or confusion. It all depended on whether she was being viewed externally or internally. It had been quite a struggle all week to not let her outer poise reflect her inner turmoil.

There was a faint and tentative knock on her door, and Shelly slowly turned her chair around. "Yes?" She had never met the neatly dressed, elderly lady at her door.

"Ms. Lowell?"

"Yes, come on in, Ms...?" She felt bad that she wasn't able to recall the woman's name. Shelly was relatively certain her visitor was an employee, because she'd seen her around the executive floor before.

"My name is Virginia. I don't have an appointment, but I was wondering if you had a few minutes free. Your secretary must have stepped away for a moment. I could come back later if you're busy..." she added hesitantly as if she was having second thoughts about being there at all.

"That's okay, Virginia. I don't have any other appointments this afternoon, and I told Nancy she could have the afternoon off." Shelly stood, walked across her office and greeted Virginia with a firm handshake. "Come on in and sit down."

The older woman glanced over her shoulder as if to check that no one was witnessing this meeting. Satisfied that the hallways were empty, she followed Shelly into the office and sat on one of the wing chairs.

Shelly decided not to put the desk between them, but sat in the other chair next to Virginia's. "Would you like something to drink?" she asked, trying to put her guest at ease.

"No, I'm fine." Her hands were clenched in her lap, and she was obviously struggling with how to begin what she'd come to say.

Shelly softened her words with a smile. "What can I help you with?"

Virginia's fingers entwined and separated several times before she finally turned toward Shelly and blurted out, "If Jim knew I was here he'd be furious—"

Abruptly straightening in her chair, Shelly interrupted. "Jim! What's this have to do with Jim?"

"I'm sure he'd fire me if he found out about this, but there's something I think you should know."

The woman cleared her throat nervously and again slid a quick look toward the door. Shelly got up and shut the door, allowing Virginia all the privacy she might feel she needed. "Go ahead. No one will ever know about this meeting but you and me."

The other woman managed a weak smile, then began. "I've been Jim's personal secretary since he came to work here almost ten years ago. I know him pretty well, I think, probably better than almost anyone else in the company."

Shelly tried to reassure her. "I thought I recognized you. Sorry I haven't been down to meet you yet, but I'm slowly making my rounds through the building."

"That's okay. I'm sure this is all pretty strange to you."

"Yes, it is." Shelly nodded ruefully. "But thank goodness there are so many excellent employees here. Everyone's making my transition a lot easier than it could have been."

Virginia sat back and relaxed as she continued. "I've heard your biggest problem is Jim. Which is unfortunate because, if you two were working together, goodness knows how successful TPRR would be."

Shelly wasn't certain how to respond without revealing her feelings, either positive or negative, for Jim, so she remained silent.

"Anyway, like I said, no one knows Jim like I do, and I just feel so sorry for him." Virginia paused, a worried frown ruffling her brow.

"Is something wrong with Jim? Isn't he at work today?" Shelly asked, her own concern growing.

"Oh, he's here. Or he was. I think he went home early, but that's not it. It's just that he's been in such turmoil over his father's will . . . and you. He isn't acting rationally, if you ask me." Virginia looked at Shelly expectantly, as if waiting for her to respond in some manner.

Shelly didn't know what was expected of her, but she finally asked, "What do you mean he isn't acting rationally?"

The secretary shifted uncomfortably in her seat as she answered, "He's so upset that he actually hired a private investigator to help him prove his father was incompetent when he rewrote his will." She heaved a long sigh of relief. "There. I said it."

"Virginia, why are you telling me this? I certainly have no control over Jim. Besides, what could I do to stop him?" Shelly asked as she lifted her hands helplessly.

"I don't know." She shook her head, and her shoulders slumped as if she'd expected Shelly to have some sort of magical solution. "He even had his personal attorney come in, and they talked about how to contest the will in court."

"I appreciate your confidence in me and your concern for Jim, but I still don't see what you think I should do, or even why you are telling me this."

"Because," Virginia said in a low voice, "I don't think Jim really wants to go through with this. He may not like what his father did or how things worked out, but I think he—" Her expression softened, but she was clearly wondering how to finish the sentence.

"He what?" Shelly prompted.

"He loves you. I've *never* seen him act like he does when he talks about you. I don't know what happened between the two of you, but he's been a very different man this week."

Shelly wasn't as convinced that it was love that had made Jim act differently. Perhaps he just wasn't used to not getting everything he wanted whenever he wanted it. She suspected she was one of the few women who had broken off with him, instead of the other way around. But she knew Virginia's intentions were honorable, and she reached out and touched the other woman's hand. "I know it wasn't easy for you to come here."

The secretary gripped Shelly's hand and insisted fervently, "You've got to do something to help Jim get through this rough period in his life. He's lost his father, his father's company and his family home, and he's losing the battle over this Mexico thing. But most of all, he's lost you." Virginia's eyes had filled with tears.

"I haven't seen him lose much of his fighting spirit over this expansion proposal of his," Shelly responded. "But you have to understand my position. I have obligations to Sam's friends and the employees of this company to do the right thing. Sam is trusting me not to let personal feelings get in the way of business decisions.''

Virginia stood up and smoothed her hair back into its meticulously neat bun. After a pause she spoke again. ''I know you have your priorities. I really do understand that. But you also have a man who loves you. If only all this stuff wasn't between you two. Maybe he had the wrong motives at first, but I think he's being honest now.'' She shrugged as she started for the door. ''Anyway, thanks for listening to me. I guess I thought you'd care. Please don't tell Jim I was here. Please,'' she pleaded.

''You were never here,'' Shelly confirmed with a conspiratorial smile. ''And I do care. I'm just not sure what I can do to change things. But thanks for telling me.''

Shelly walked over to the door and gently closed it after Virginia left. She didn't usually like to isolate herself in her office, but in the peace and solitude she could think more clearly about what she should do. How could she balance the demands of the company, her feelings toward Jim and her instinctive competitiveness? And what about Emily? Shelly had an obligation to provide for her daughter in the best way she knew how.

Things had not been easy for them, and Emily had never had any of the little extras all her friends had. Until now. She loved living at the ranch and having horses to ride and lots of other pets around. She was old enough to need her own room and a mother who didn't have to spend all night waiting on tables, hoping there would be enough tips to pay for a new pair of tennis shoes.

And Shelly was enjoying the security of knowing all her bills were paid off and that she had some money in the bank. This was not the job she'd always dreamed of having, but she was enjoying the challenge. And someday maybe a man would enter her life...a man she could love and trust...a man who was more interested in her than in regaining what he felt was his inheritance.

And always the thought that niggled in the back of her mind intruded. It *was* his birthright. Just because he and his father hadn't been seeing eye-to-eye the day Sam died shouldn't have taken it all away. Shelly knew how upset she'd be if someone cheated her or her daughter out of what they felt was rightly theirs.

She rubbed her throbbing temples with her fingertips and leaned on the edge of her desk. There were so many conflicting demands on her that she just wanted to escape. Run away from all the pressures and worries and questions... even if just for a day. Well, why not?

She looked at her calendar and confirmed that there was nothing else scheduled for the rest of the day. Shelly considered her options for a moment, then called down to the receptionist. "If anyone wants me, tell them I had to do something with my daughter. I'm leaving for the rest of the day. I'll be back in my office first thing Monday morning."

With a much lighter heart she retrieved her coat and purse, then switched off the lights in her office. She deliberately left behind her briefcase, which had become a permanent fixture since assuming her new role. This weekend belonged to herself and her daughter.

The showdown on Monday would arrive soon enough.

SHELLY AND EMILY walked out the front door of Emily's school hand in hand.

"This is such a nice surprise, Mama. It'll be neat for it to be just you and me."

"I needed some time with my best friend," Shelly said as she squeezed Emily's hand firmly. "I thought we'd go shopping first and then have dinner together. Is that okay?"

"Yeah. Sounds great. Can we eat at that Chinese restaurant? I've never eaten Chinese food, but Tricia says it's great."

"Sure. It's your choice."

"Oh, but I promised to practice the play at Jennifer's later."

"That's fine. I'll drop you by there after we eat."

Shelly and Emily walked to their Bronco, which was parked in front of the school, and got in. It took them only a few minutes to arrive at the small shopping mall.

At first Emily was hesitant to show an interest in a blouse or a pair of jeans. But Shelly encouraged her daughter to pick out a couple of new outfits, and the girl soon got into the spirit of the moment and practically ran from rack to rack, trying to choose. She'd never had the freedom to pick anything she wanted, but her common sense held her selections to clothing that was both reasonably priced and serviceable.

As Shelly watched her daughter make these tough decisions, her heart swelled with pride. Emily was a good kid, intelligent, levelheaded and yet, still able to laugh with childlike pleasure at the silliest things. It was nice to be able to provide some little unexpected extras for her daughter.

They left their packages in the back seat of the Bronco and walked to the Chinese restaurant that was located next to the mall. It wasn't crowded yet, even though it was a Friday evening, so they were seated immediately. They ordered two different dinners, then shared them while Emily chattered on about her friends and what had been going on in school. When the food was all gone and there was a lapse in the conversation, Shelly asked, "Did you have fun tonight?"

Emily smiled. "It was great. Thanks, Mama." But then her expression grew solemn.

"Something wrong?" Shelly asked.

"I was just wondering whatever happened to Jim?"

Shelly was surprised by the question. Not since the day after she'd fled from his apartment and she'd told her daughter Jim wouldn't be around anymore had Emily brought him up. "Why do you ask?"

"I miss him. He was a lot of fun, and he really helped me with my lines. I thought he said he'd practice some more with me."

Shelly turned her attention to the check the waiter had just left on the table, as she tried to think of a simple way to explain to Emily the pain of broken relationships. Even though the girl wasn't too young to understand the value of trust and honesty, the wounds were still too fresh for Shelly to objectively discuss them. Instead she finally admitted, "I miss him, too, Emily. We did have some good times, didn't we?"

Emily tilted her head to one side as she studied her mother's face.

"What?" Shelly asked when her daughter didn't comment.

"I wish you'd go out with him again. Maybe you could invite him to my play."

Shelly pulled her wallet from her purse and counted out enough money to cover the check and a suitable tip. As she began to slide across the booth to get up from the table, she looked at the girl. "I wouldn't count on Jim being at your play Monday night, Emily. He and I were very angry when we decided not to date anymore. I don't think he'll want anything to do with me."

Emily's face showed her disappointment. But her words showed it wasn't only for herself. "Too bad, Mama. He made you laugh, and you hardly ever laughed before."

Shelly had no response. In fact, she knew if she tried to speak at that moment, she would probably have embarrassed herself by breaking into tears. So she settled for the busy act of putting on her coat and helping Emily with hers before leaving the restaurant.

It was almost eight o'clock when Shelly dropped Emily off at Jennifer's house with a promise to pick her up around eleven. Shelly didn't want to go back to the empty ranch house, so she stopped at the multiplex and bought a ticket to a movie she'd been wanting to see.

Loaded down with popcorn and a soft drink, she found a seat in the back of the theater. All around her couples were laughing and talking, holding hands and enjoying the evening together. Several times she even thought she saw Jim with a date, but it always turned out to be two strangers...much to her relief. Never had she felt so alone, and she was profoundly glad when the lights finally dimmed and the movie began.

It was an interesting movie, quickly pulling her into the plot and the relationship of the characters, giving her temporary relief from her own thoughts and problems. But as the lights brightened and the couples began leaving, two by two, she was thrust back into reality.

It was still too early to get Emily, so Shelly decided a cup of hot coffee and a visit with an old friend would hit the spot perfectly.

The last car pulled out onto the highway from the Silver Spur parking area as Shelly drove into the lot. As she got out of her car and walked briskly to the front door, the cold, late-night air instantly penetrated her wool coat and sent a stampede of goose bumps racing along her skin. The familiar bell rang as she entered, and Shelly went to the counter and slapped her open palm down on it loudly. "Where's the service around this place?"

"Shelly!" exclaimed Clara as she looked up from the grill she was scraping. "How've you been? It's so good to see you."

Shelly rushed into the kitchen and gave Clara a big hug. "It's good to see you, too, Clara. I never thought I'd miss this place, but I do."

Clara looked at the young woman who was now wearing Shelly's old waitress uniform and said, "Where're my manners? Shelly, this is Kim Masters.

Kim, this is Shelly Lowell. She used to be our night waitress."

"Nice to meet you," Kim said as she extended her right hand for a handshake. "Clara's told me all about you. Wow! Getting all that money must have been pretty exciting."

"It's not as great as it sounds," responded Shelly as she shook Kim's hand firmly.

"Can I get you anything?" The young waitress stared at Shelly with awe.

"It sounds strange to be on the other end of that question, but yes, how about a piece of lemon pie and a cup of coffee?" Shelly hugged Clara again. "I've missed talking to you."

"I know what you mean. Let's go over and sit down for a while and catch up on the news." Clara walked over to the corner booth where she and Shelly had spent many a night talking away the hours.

Shelly sat in her usual place facing the front window, where she'd always been able to see any customers first. Old habits were hard to break. As she settled into the booth, she gave Clara an exasperated look and sighed. "Life was so much simpler back here."

"Yeah," Clara responded. "I'll bet that's true. At least here if you have a problem customer, he'd be gone in an hour at the most."

"Boy if that isn't the truth," Shelly agreed with a wry smile.

Kim walked over and set the coffee and pie on the table, then returned to the counter.

Shelly sat and stirred some sugar into her coffee, then took a small bite of the thick, frothy meringue. While it tasted familiar and was as good as ever, it didn't increase her appetite, something that had been lacking for the last week. If it hadn't been for Emily, Shelly probably wouldn't have eaten anything, because nothing appealed to her.

It was that obnoxious Jim, she thought. If he wasn't dominating her time at work because of the preparation and research required to acquaint herself with the expansion, he was sneaking into her dreams, both waking and sleeping. He'd seemed so perfect, but now she knew that was all part of his act. Of course he'd been able to help Emily with her play—he was a terrific actor. He'd sure fooled the two Lowell women.

Shelly put her fork down and took another sip of the hot coffee. It felt good after being outside in the frosty winter night.

"Must be *some* problem for you to not eat at least two bites of that pie," commented Clara. "It's your favorite."

"It's wonderful, as usual, but..." Shelly swirled the dark liquid around in the thick china cup, watching the black whirlpool hypnotically.

"Is Emily okay? She's not sick or anything, is she?" Clara asked with growing concern.

"No, Emily's fine. She really loves it at the ranch. There are horses, chickens, a dog and even a deer that comes into the yard every evening and eats corn out of her hand." Shelly shook her head and sighed. "It's Jim. Sam's son. He's making my life miserable."

"How so?"

"Remember that man who came into the Spur while I was still working here?"

"The tall, good-looking one you told me about?"

"Yes, that's the one."

"Oh, yeah. Whatever happened to him?" Clara asked as she sat up and watched Shelly closely, giving her total attention to the story.

"That nice, sweet man turned out to be Sam's son. He came here just to find out about me and my relationship with Sam." Shelly could feel her blood pressure rising as she thought about how Jim had deceived her.

"You mean *he's* Sonny Mitchell?"

Shelly knew her expression was as miserable and embarrassed as she felt. "Yes, but I didn't find out until last week. He really played me like a fiddle...taking me out dancing and paying attention to Emily. I thought..." She paused, barely able to speak around the huge lump that had risen in her throat. "I thought he was the most wonderful man I'd ever met," she whispered in a voice almost too soft for Clara to hear.

"You didn't..." Clara gave her a pitying look that only increased Shelly's humiliation.

"I'm afraid I did," she admitted, her voice thick with regret. "I found out the next morning by accident who he really was. I was so hurt." She felt her cheeks burn at the memory, and she lifted the cup to her lips to hide her discomfort.

"Hurt? Why hurt? I'd be furious," responded Clara with sympathetic indignity.

Shelly thought back to all the good times she and Jim had had together. For that brief moment she'd been happier than she'd ever been in her whole life. "I really was falling in love with him. Emily was crazy about him, too. She doesn't understand why he's suddenly stopped coming over."

"Sounds to me like you really have it bad for this guy. Maybe there's still a chance for you two."

Shelly shook her head emphatically. "No, it's over. Actually, it never really started. I was falling in love with a man who didn't exist. All he cared about was the money, not me or Emily." She blinked rapidly, trying to hold back the tears that suddenly filled her eyes. With a sniffle she brusquely wiped the moisture away with her fingertips. "It doesn't matter."

"No way to patch things up?" asked Clara, extending her hand across the table to comfort her friend.

Again Shelly shook her head. "No, he thinks I'm a tramp, and I think he's a greedy playboy. That doesn't make such a good foundation for a relationship."

"That's an understatement." Clara rolled her eyes in agreement.

"Besides, we're on opposite sides of the fence at the railroad, too. He's really pushing for an expansion into Mexico, and I'm fighting against it." Shelly's forehead furrowed into a perplexed frown. "You know, it's funny, but I can see both sides of the issue. It does seem that TPRR would benefit financially from the project, and even though I'm sure there would be some unexpected bumps, it looks like a good idea."

"Then why are you fighting it?"

Shelly leaned back against the cracked, orange vinyl seat. "Because Sam was dead set against it, and there's no question that he knew more about that railroad than I'll ever know. I must be overlooking something . . . or Jim's playing another one of his cute little tricks on us all. He must have something to gain from the contract. Maybe they're passing him money under the table." She shrugged. "I just don't trust him."

Clara gave her an encouraging smile. "You'll figure it out. Just take your time—"

"That's another problem," Shelly interrupted. "I don't have any time. It's coming up for a vote on Monday, and if we don't settle it soon, the whole company could be in jeopardy. Some of our stockholders are getting restless, and we can't afford to lose their support if we want to do any expansion into other areas."

Shelly looked up at Clara and tried to return her smile. "Anyway, enough about me. How about you? What's new with you and John?"

"Same ol', same ol'. My husband's still sweet and lazy. I'm just glad football season's over." Clara's chuckle rumbled from deep in her oversize bosom. "And things are going pretty good around here. Pete's as ornery as ever, but he knows to keep out of my way. And Kim's working out fine, even though I doubt she'll stay here long. She goes to college during the day and has a boyfriend who's trying to get her to move to Dallas with him."

"I'd trade my life for yours in a heartbeat, Clara. If it wasn't for Emily, I'd—"

Clara interrupted. "Listen, gal. You're smart, but your emotions are getting in the way of your brains. I belong here at the Spur, but I always knew you were too good for this place. Things have been happening too fast for you lately. You need to decide what's right for you and Emily. Then go for it."

Shelly gave Clara an amused look. "Are you sure you're not Oprah in disguise?" She glanced around the small diner. "Are we on hidden camera, and this is a show about women who are easily fooled by men? You'd think I'd have learned something by mistaking a multimillionaire for a homeless bum. But no, along comes his son, and I believe his story about being a wandering cowboy. I feel like I'm on a phone-in radio talk show or something. I guess I'm not a very good judge of character."

"Sure you are. You knew Sam was a nice guy. Maybe you weren't completely wrong about his son, either."

Shelly shrugged. "We'll see who survives the battle on Monday. I may be back here begging for a job."

"Don't be such a goose. Things are going to turn out just fine."

"I wish I could be that sure."

"You come back in here on Monday night and tell me how it all turns out, okay?"

Two tractor trailer trucks had parked outside, and their drivers entered the diner in a burst of cold air.

"Hey, Clara, where's that coffee? We're freezing out there," one of them declared.

"Hey, look, it's Shelly. How's it going, babe?" another asked, when he noticed her sitting across from Clara.

"Fine, Harry. I see you're still dragging that ugly trailer around," Shelly teased. "When're you going to get that thing painted? Maybe a nice landscape?"

He waved away her suggestion with a laugh, as he followed the others to a table.

Shelly slid out of the booth and stood. "I guess I'd better get going. Emily's practicing the play at her friend's house, but I'm supposed to pick her up at eleven."

"Well, anytime you need to talk, stop in. Don't be such a stranger, you hear?" demanded Clara as she, too, lumbered to her feet.

"Yes, ma'am. I hear," Shelly replied with a genuine smile, her first in days. "You always were able to cheer me up. And I want you and your husband to come out to the ranch for dinner one night. I'll call next week and set up a time. Oh, by the way, there's an opening for a mechanic in the locomotive shop. If John's interested, tell him to let me know."

"I'm sure he'd love to get back on at the railroad," responded Clara with more enthusiasm than Shelly had ever seen her muster. "And we'd love to come to dinner. I miss Emily. I got used to having her around, always underfoot."

Shelly put on her coat, knowing that Clara's gruffness was all an act. The truth was the older woman was Shelly's best friend in this small town. She walked to the front door, saying goodbye to Kim at the counter. With a final smile and wave at Clara, Shelly left the Spur and headed to Jennifer's house to pick Emily up before going home, where she knew she would toss and turn all night. She had only two days left to decide the fate of the TPRR—as well as her own.

Chapter Thirteen

The executive boardroom was filled to capacity as again Shelly and Harlan were the last ones to arrive. She looked around the room as everyone conversed with the people next to them, talking about their weekend or the score of last night's Mavericks' basketball game. It hardly seemed like the battleground she knew it would have to become that day, if the TPRR were to move on.

She went directly to the big chair at the head of the table, sat down and arranged several folders in front of her. She was very aware of Jim sitting a few chairs down on her right, but she forced herself not to look directly at him. She had plans for this meeting and didn't want her expression to give anything away too soon.

"Are we ready to go?" asked Harlan in a loud voice.

The people were slow to respond as if reluctant to leap into the fracas that was likely to ensue, once discussion of the expansion began. Harlan interrupted them again, more insistently. "People, we need to get going. I doubt that any of us want to stay here all day." With that the room grew quiet. Harlan turned to Shelly and said, "Shelly? It's all yours."

"Today we are faced with a very important decision. It will shape our future economically and politically for years to come. I know each of you has an interest in the outcome of this decision. Everyone will get a chance to speak. I've asked Harlan to act as the timekeeper and if need be, the sergeant at arms."

Nervous laughter could be heard as several people looked at their watches.

"Harlan," Shelly said as she glanced in his direction.

"The basic issue," Harlan began, "is whether or not we are going to enter into a twenty-year contract with the Mexican Government to provide rail service across the border." Harlan looked around the room at each member. "I'll open the floor for discussion."

While questions were asked, then answered by various members of the board, Jim sat quietly, studying the faces of the members. Shelly knew he'd met individually with every member prior to the meeting, and he probably had a better idea of how the vote would go than she did. Silently she urged him to speak up, to defend his proposal, to justify the risks and convince everyone that the expansion would be the best thing that could ever happen to the TPRR. Why didn't he? *Come on, Jim ... take over the meeting.* She tried to send the message telepathically down the table to the man who was focusing on his legal pad, idly making circular doodles in the border.

Finally, when there was a lull in the discussion, Jim looked up. Slowly he rose to his feet and leaned forward on the table, forcing everyone to meet his gaze as he glanced from one person to the next. "Many of you've known me since I was a kid. Some of you still think I'm a kid. But I've worked hard to get this business negotiated for our railroad. I think we're all very aware of the issues here, and we could spend all day talking about the exchange rate and the exclusivity clauses and where any arbitration would be tried. It's obvious you've all done extensive research on this...especially Ms. Lowell." Jim nodded in her direction and gave her a faint smile.

"Thanks," Shelly said as she smiled and nodded back at him. *Yes, here's your chance... go for it,* she silently encouraged.

Looking around the room again, Jim spoke calmly but passionately. "But aside from her financial concerns, I ask you to keep in mind what my father created here. Our railroad was built on risk taking. Many times there were no contracts, and decisions were based on gut feelings and handshakes. Sam Mitchell started this company on his sweat and dreams. All I ask of you now is to support me and my dreams to continue that tradition. You know *my* vote, Ms. Lowell. I'll leave you people to do the right thing." Jim walked to the head of the table. He stopped next to her and reached into his pocket. Drawing out an envelope from inside his suit coat pocket, he handed it to Shelly. His expression was strangely wistful, but held no hostility as he said, "The best man won. Congratulations." Without another word he held his head high as he walked to the door, opened it and left.

Everyone's shocked gazes followed him. But as the door shut firmly behind him, they turned back until those gazes were focused on her. Shelly glanced around, then at the envelope in her hands. Her hands trembled as she opened it and she quickly scanned its contents. *Oh no, Jim, why?* she cried to herself. But aloud she whispered to Harlan, "He's resigned his position with the company and given up all claims to his father's properties."

Usually so unflappable, even Harlan was unable to hide his surprise. "I guess that'll make today's decision a lot easier."

Shelly shook her head. "No, it ruins everything."

Harlan gave her a confused look, then asked loudly, "Are we ready to vote?"

As the people in the room began to talk to one another in hushed speculation, Shelly whispered, "Harlan, I don't want to go through with this vote today."

"What?" Harlan asked incredulously. "What do you mean you don't want to go through with the vote today? Why not? With Sonny gone, it's guaranteed to fail."

"I know," she answered. "And I'm not sure I want it to fail. In fact, if I had to vote, right this minute, I'd vote yes because I think Jim is right."

"You do?" Harlan's eyes widened behind his round metal-framed spectacles.

"Yes." She paused, wishing fervently that things had gone differently. "You see, I was going to let him lead today's discussion and swing the vote." She took an envelope out of her own pocket and waved it in front of Harlan. "I was going to offer my resignation to him and allow him to take back his father's company after he'd roused everyone's support. But now I can't." She pressed her lips together as she tried to think of her next move. "He beat me to the punch.

How can I relinquish control to a man who's just quit?"

Harlan was staring at her as if she'd suddenly grown two heads. She said to him, "Postpone the vote. Call out for pizza. Start up a poker game. Frankly, right this minute I don't care. You handle it. I've got to see Jim." Shelly got up and hurried out of the room.

She didn't wait for the elevator, but practically ran down the two flights of stairs, then on to Jim's office. Rounding the corner, she stopped in front of Virginia's desk. "Is Jim in his office?" she asked.

"No, Shelly. He came back, grabbed his coat and briefcase and left. Is something wrong?" the woman asked.

"He left the meeting before we could vote, and he . . . well, I think he's making a huge mistake. I need to talk with him right away. Any idea where he went?" she asked anxiously.

"None. In fact he said he wouldn't be back. I assume he meant today—"

"No, I think he meant forever." Shelly rubbed her forehead, pushing her bangs back from her face in a show of frustration.

Virginia gasped, her face blanching in surprise.

"If he calls or comes back, please call me at home right away, okay?" Shelly scribbled down her phone number, then added the number of the car phone, too. "Oh . . . and don't spread the word just yet. I'm hoping he'll change his mind before things go too far."

She stopped at her office, picked up her coat and purse, then said to her secretary, "I'm going home if anyone needs me. But it had better be important, because my daughter's in a play tonight and I've got to

finish making her costume." As she walked to the
Bronco in the parking lot, she realized she still had
Jim's letter of resignation in her hand. Once inside the
vehicle, she set her things on the seat, then neatly
folded Jim's letter and placed it in her purse next to
her own.

THE SCHOOL AUDITORIUM was filled with parents and
relatives. Cameras and video camcorders were everywhere. No one wanted to miss their child's opening
and closing night. Shelly and Emily walked into the
hallway outside the front of the auditorium together.
Still upset by the day's events, Shelly tried not to let
her bad attitude affect the evening's festivities. "You
look great, honey. I can't wait to see you perform."

"I'm *really* nervous, Mama. What if I forget my
lines? What if I don't come onstage at the right time,
or—"

"Stop worrying," Shelly reassured her. "You've
been over your part so many times you've worn the
print off the pages. You're going to do great, and even
if you mess up a little, that's okay. Everyone's going
to see how pretty you look in this outfit, and they
won't even notice any boo-boos." She looked down at
the small camera in her hands. "I just wish I had a
video camera instead of this. I'd love to have your
stage debut on tape forever."

"Well, if I forget my lines, at least no one will know
if there's just a picture to look at." Emily smiled and
hugged her mother.

"You'd better get backstage. Break a leg, honey."

"What?" Emily looked shocked.

"It's a theater tradition. It means 'good luck,' but I think they believe it's bad luck to actually wish someone good luck," Shelly tried to explain, but succeeded in confusing even herself.

"Gee, actors are kind of strange, aren't they?"

"Yes, I guess they are." Shelly took her daughter's coat, then gave her a gentle push toward the back-stage door. "Now get going before they send out a search party for the fairy godmother."

Emily ran off down the side hall, her wings flopping up and down as she moved. Shelly waited until her daughter was safely inside the door, then she entered the auditorium and worked her way forward to get as close to center stage as possible.

Moments after she found a seat in the middle of the fifth row, the school principal walked out onstage and welcomed the parents and guests to the evening's performance. The lights dimmed, and the curtain opened.

As THE APPLAUSE died down, the audience stood and began talking proudly about the budding Thespians in their families as they left the auditorium. Shelly walked to the left aisle and joined the crowd that was slowly moving toward the back. Suddenly she saw Jim, towering over the people around him as he left the theater.

She tried to push her way to the back, hoping to have a chance to talk to him. She'd tried all afternoon to track him down, but not even his friend Boomer had been able to help her. He either hadn't returned to his apartment or was refusing to answer his door, and his phone must have been intentionally left off the hook because it registered busy all day. With each passing hour it became more obvious that he didn't want to discuss the matter with her or anyone else. She certainly hadn't expected to see him here tonight, and if she could catch him . . .

But by the time she arrived in the hallway outside the back of the auditorium, Jim had disappeared.

Shelly didn't hurry to get backstage because she knew her daughter would be busy with her friends. So she waited outside the door with the other parents until their fairy-tale characters came out. There was so much noise and confusion that Shelly didn't even notice her daughter until she felt a hand grip her arm.

"How was I?"

Shelly, who had turned, half-expecting to see Jim's face in front of her, had to drop her gaze to the same level as her daughter's excited voice. "You were great sweetheart. I was so impressed!"

"I didn't forget my lines, either." Emily seemed so excited about her flawless performance.

"I know. I was saying them right along with you." Shelly laughed. "And I took lots of pictures."

Emily twirled around, obviously delighted at the way the soft satin and crisp net, sprinkled liberally with sequins, sparkled in the artificial light. When she stopped, Shelly noticed for the first time that Emily was holding a single red rose with streamers of ribbons trailing from it.

"Where'd you get the rose?" she asked, glancing around at the other children and noticing that none of them had one.

"Oh, Jim gave it to me." Emily lifted it to her nose and took a deep breath. "Wasn't that sweet of him?"

"When did you see Jim?"

"He came backstage after the show. He said he wanted me to know how proud he was that I'd done so good. He brought his video camera and said he'd mail me a copy of the tape."

Shelly's gaze quickly scanned the crowd but didn't find Jim among the few remaining adults. "Damn," she muttered under her breath.

"What did you say?"

"I said I'm sorry I missed him. I was hoping..." Shelly sighed and blinked back a rush of tears that had filled her eyes. Who would have guessed that Jim was so thoughtful to touch a child's heart at such a critical moment? Actually, it wasn't so surprising. The Jim Shelly had first gotten to know would have done it in a minute. It was the Jim-Sonny personality she hadn't liked.

"Didn't you promise to take me to the Spur to celebrate?" Emily reminded her mother. The child couldn't quite stand still as the adrenaline raced through her small body.

"Yes, I did. And if you'll put on your coat, we'll head on over there so you can tell Clara all about your performance."

"I wish we could stop by Jim's apartment. His hot chocolate's better than the Spur's," Emily commented with an innocent look in her sparkling blue eyes.

Shelly looked at her hopeful expression. "I'm sure Jim has other plans tonight. Come on, let's go before Clara sells all the pie."

Shelly and Emily, hand in hand, walked through the front doors of the school and found their Bronco in the parking lot. She looked around but didn't see either Jim's black Corvette or that old beat-up truck he'd borrowed.

The drive to the Spur took only a few minutes. Emily was till hyper from the excitement and bounced out of the Bronco as soon as they parked.

Clara saw them enter and rushed to the front door with an order pad and pen extended in Emily's direction. "May I have your autograph, Miss Lowell?" Clara asked seriously.

"Oh, Clara. Stop fooling around," Emily said, almost embarrassed. But she took the pad and automatically fell back on her well-taught penmanship, as she carefully wrote her name in precise script across the yellow paper.

"She was spectacular tonight, Clara. You should have seen her. She played her part perfectly," Shelly said proudly.

"She looks like she's ready to bounce off the ceiling," Clara observed wryly.

"Oh, she's starting to calm down now. You should have seen her right after the show." Shelly hung their coats on the rack and sat on one of the bar stools. "We'd like some hot chocolate, please."

"On the way," Clara said as she headed for the kitchen.

"Where's Kim tonight?"

Clara answered, "She wasn't feeling well, so I told her I'd cover for her. Interested in working tonight, kid?"

"No, thanks. I had a hard day today," responded Shelly with an exhausted sigh.

Emily, her magic wand still clenched in her hand, scrambled up on the stool next to her mother and asked, "Do you have any doughnuts left?"

"Just what you need," Clara commented with gruff affection, "more sugar." But she had two glazed doughnuts on a small plate with her when she returned.

"Here we go, ladies. Hot chocolate." Clara set the cups on the counter and placed the doughnuts in front of Emily, then pulled up a stool and sat across from them.

Shelly, Emily and Clara talked for nearly an hour, interrupted occasionally by customers. Every time the bell rang, Emily would look around expectantly, then return to her hot chocolate with a look of disappointment.

Finally Shelly glanced at her watch and exclaimed, "It's almost midnight. We'd better get going."

Emily shook her head emphatically. "No, not yet. I'm still too excited and—" she glanced toward the door "—thirsty." She held out her empty cup toward Clara. "Could I have another one, please?"

"Oh no, it's late," Shelly answered, taking the cup and setting it aside. "You have school tomorrow, young lady, and you're going to be dead on your feet." Shelly reached for her purse and slid off the stool.

The front door to the Spur opened and the familiar bell rang, signaling the arrival of another late-night customer.

Jim stepped into the Spur and let the door shut behind him, hitting the bell again as it closed. He walked slowly toward the counter and stopped a couple of feet behind Shelly. When Emily looked around, a smile of pure delight stretched across her young face.

"You came!" she exclaimed. "I was hoping you would."

"How could I not after you gave me such a nice invitation?" he asked.

Shelly whirled around, apparently recognizing his voice. Her mouth opened, but no words came out.

"I brought a copy for you," he said, holding out a videotape to Emily. "Your grandkids will be so proud of you when they see this about fifty years from now."

"Why?" Shelly finally managed to ask.

"Why what?" Jim was annoyed at the quaver in his voice. He'd wanted to be so cool, but just standing this close to her was affecting his equilibrium. As he watched the variety of emotions clearly displayed in her eyes, he wanted nothing more than to pull her into his arms and hold her tight. It had been so long since he'd touched her. But there were still a few things that needed to be discussed, to be settled, before they could decide whether or not to move to the next step—or to call it quits forever.

He hoped that last option wouldn't be her choice, even though he knew she had many reasons to keep him out of her life. For the first time he was willing to do whatever it took to change her mind. All the pride and cockiness that had been so much a part of his character was gone. The only thing that was important to him now was that he somehow make Shelly understand . . . and hopefully forgive him.

"Why did you go to the play tonight? I tried to catch up with you afterward," Shelly commented as a guarded look dropped over her expressive eyes.

"I wanted to see how my protégée did." He turned to Emily. "And you made me proud."

Emily threw her arms around his neck and gave him a big hug. "Thanks. I remembered everything you told me, and it really helped."

Clara, apparently sensing that Jim and Shelly had things they needed to discuss privately, took Emily's hand. "Why don't you help me in the kitchen for a minute? You could make the biscuit dough for breakfast while I clean the grill."

Emily's eyes brightened and she hopped off the stool. "Sure."

After they'd disappeared into the kitchen, Shelly reached into her purse and pulled out an envelope that looked very much like the one he'd given her. Solemnly she handed it to him.

"I guess you've talked to Harlan?" she asked.

"No," he answered with a shake of his head. "I haven't spoken to anyone. How'd the vote go?"

"We didn't vote. Or at least, I don't think they did. I left the meeting early, too."

"You did? Why?"

"If you'd stuck around, you'd have found out for yourself," she retorted. "Anyway, I'd already decided to vote for the expansion, then to turn the company back over to you." She nodded toward the envelope. "My resignation's in there, along with my agreement to sign over the titles to the ranch and everything else your father left me."

"Why would you do that?"

Shelly's smile was tinged with melancholy. "It was fun while it lasted. But just like Cinderella, the ball ended, and all the beautiful horses turned back to mice and the golden carriage back into a pumpkin." She shrugged. "It wasn't ever really mine. Your father probably changed his will in a moment of anger or loneliness or whatever. But it really should have gone to you."

Jim looked down at the envelope in his hand and realized just how much he was holding. It was everything he'd ever hoped for or dreamed of... until he'd met Shelly.

"All I'm asking," she continued, unaware of the sadness raging inside him, "is that you let me keep the Bronco and ten thousand dollars. I've always wanted to get a college degree in education or maybe business administration. My weeks as an executive were very interesting, but I realize now that I have a lot to learn before I can hope to take over a whole company."

Jim started to speak, but Shelly hurried to add, "Oh, and I used some money to pay my bills, but I had a note drawn up. If you have no objections, I'll start paying you back in four years after I've graduated and gotten a—"

"No!" he interrupted firmly.

Shelly, who had yet to meet his gaze, lifted her face until she was staring into his eyes. "No? You mean, you won't let me borrow the money? But—"

"No, I mean you can't borrow it because I don't have the authority to loan it to you." He held up the envelope and deliberately tore it in half, then in quarters. "My father meant for you to have it, and it's all yours." He laughed out loud, suddenly feeling freer and happier than he had in years. "It's funny. I thought this was what I wanted out of life. But I realized that all of it meant nothing without love.''

"Love?" she echoed weakly.

"Yes, love. And you, lovely lady, taught me everything I know about it. You and Emily, that is.''

"But, I thought..."

"Yes, I know what you thought, and I'm truly sorry. I would do anything to be able to go back to the beginning and start over.'' He reached out and let his fingers trail tenderly along the curve of her jawline. "But I can't, so I'll just have to try, for the rest of my life, to make it up to you. If you'll let me.'' His eyes softened as he looked down into her beloved face. "Shelly, I promise I'll never lie to you again. I love you, and I'm hoping you love me...at least a little bit.''

Shelly hesitated and his heart stopped. He didn't know what he would do if she refused to give him a second chance. Oh, well. He was young. He had at least forty more years to try to get her to change her mind.

But then she lifted her arms and threw them around his neck, and he knew he wouldn't have to wait that long. "Oh yes, Jim, I do love you. The thought of life without you was—''

Before she could say anything else, he leaned down and captured her lips in a long-overdue kiss. He wrapped his arms around her and hugged her tightly, never ever wanting to let her go.

They kissed again and again and held each other for many moments. Finally she stepped away just enough so she could reach into her purse and pull out the envelope he recognized as the one holding his resignation. "I can't accept your resignation, Jim." Shelly then proceeded to tear it up and drop it to the floor.

"Why not? I meant it," Jim insisted. "I realize I'm asking you to marry a man who has no job and no visible means of income, but I'll find something."

She leveled a severe look at him. "Would you quit being so stubborn? It doesn't matter who owns the company, it's going to need someone with railroad experience to run it. And that person isn't me."

"I don't want any misunderstandings about the TPRR to come between you and me."

"I agree," Shelly stated. "The way I figure it, I can go to college and you can take over the company. That way we can still keep it in the family." She smiled as Jim grabbed her and pulled her so close that her feet left the floor.

Through the pass-through window, he could see Clara and Emily listening raptly, making no effort not to eavesdrop. When she saw he was looking at her, Emily grinned broadly and gave him an enthusiastic thumbs-up. Behind Shelly's back, Jim returned the gesture and added a wink.

With his arm still around Shelly, they walked to the jukebox in the corner of the diner. Reaching into his pocket, he extracted a quarter and deposited it into the slot. He pushed two buttons, and the old machine once again cranked out a tune. As Emily waved her magic wand in time to the music, Shelly and Jim began dancing to the simple but poignant words of "I Cross My Heart." On the wall, the old-fashioned clock that had long ago been rescued from the local train station announced the arrival of midnight with twelve long chimes.

Emily ran out, and Jim gathered her up with one arm while still holding Shelly close. The three of them whirled around the room, dancing in the beginning of a new day.

And they lived happily ever after . . . together.

Once in a while, there's a story so special, a story so
unusual, that your pulse races, your blood rushes.
We call this

Borrowed Time is one such book.

Kathleen Welles receives a most unusual offer: to sell one past day in her life for a
million dollars! What she didn't realize was that she'd be transported back in time, to
the very day she'd sold—the day she lost her true love, Zachary Forest. Can she right
her wrongs and reclaim the man she loves in a mere twenty-four hours?

#574 BORROWED TIME
by
Cassie Miles

Available in March, wherever Harlequin books are sold.
Watch for more Heartbeat stories, coming your way soon!

Take 4 bestselling love stories FREE

Plus get a FREE surprise gift!

Special Limited-time Offer

Mail to Harlequin Reader Service®

3010 Walden Avenue
P.O. Box 1867
Buffalo, N.Y. 14269-1867

YES! Please send me 4 free Harlequin American Romance® novels and my free surprise gift. Then send me 4 brand-new novels every month, which I will receive months before they appear in bookstores. Bill me at the low price of $2.89 each plus 25¢ delivery and applicable sales tax, if any.* That's the complete price and a savings of over 10% off the cover prices—quite a bargain! I understand that accepting the books and gift places me under no obligation ever to buy any books. I can always return a shipment and cancel at any time. Even if I never buy another book from Harlequin, the 4 free books and the surprise gift are mine to keep forever.

154 BPA ANRL

Name _____ (PLEASE PRINT)

Address _____ Apt. No. _____

City _____ State _____ Zip _____

This offer is limited to one order per household and not valid to present Harlequin American Romance® subscribers. *Terms and prices are subject to change without notice. Sales tax applicable in N.Y.

UAM-295   ©1990 Harlequin Enterprises Limited

He's at home in denim; she's bathed in diamonds...
Her tastes run to peanut butter; his to pâté...
They're bound to be together...

for Richer, for Poorer

We're delighted to bring you more of the kinds of stories you love,
in FOR RICHER, FOR POORER—a miniseries in which lovers
are drawn together by passion...but separated by price!

Next month, look for

#575 RYAN'S BRIDE
Julie Kistler

Don't miss any of the FOR RICHER, FOR POORER
books, coming to you in the months ahead—
only from American Romance!

HARLEQUIN® AMERICAN ROMANCE®

IS BRINGING YOU A BABY BOOM!

NEW ARRIVALS

We're expecting! This spring, from March through May, three very special Harlequin American Romance authors invite you to read about three equally special heroines—all of whom are on a nine-month adventure! We expect each soon-to-be mom will find the man of her dreams—and a daddy in the bargain!

So don't miss the first of these titles:

#576 BABY MAKES NINE
by Vivian Leiber
March 1995

Look for the New Arrivals logo—and please help us welcome our new arrivals!

NA-G

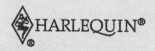

Harlequin invites you to the most
romantic wedding of the season.

Rope the cowboy of your dreams in
Marry Me, Cowboy!

A collection of 4 brand-new stories,
celebrating weddings, written by:

New York Times bestselling author

JANET DAILEY

and favorite authors

Margaret Way
Anne McAllister
Susan Fox

Be sure not to miss Marry Me, Cowboy!
coming this April

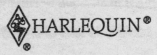 HARLEQUIN®

MMC

Fifty red-blooded, white-hot, true-blue hunks
from every State in the Union!

Look for MEN MADE IN AMERICA! Written by some
of our most popular authors, these stories feature some
of the strongest, sexiest men, each from a different state
in the union!

Two titles available every month at your favorite
retail outlet.

In February, look for:

THE SECURITY MAN by Dixie Browning
(North Carolina)
A CLASS ACT by Kathleen Eagle (North Dakota)

In March, look for:

TOO NEAR THE FIRE by Lindsay McKenna (Ohio)
A TIME AND A SEASON by Curtiss Ann Matlock
(Oklahoma)

You won't be able to resist MEN MADE IN AMERICA!

HARLEQUIN®

Don't miss these Harlequin favorites by some of our most distinguished authors! And now, you can receive a discount by ordering two or more titles!

HT#25577	WILD LIKE THE WIND by Janice Kaiser	$2.99	☐
HT#25589	THE RETURN OF CAINE O'HALLORAN by JoAnn Ross	$2.99	☐
HP#11626	THE SEDUCTION STAKES by Lindsay Armstrong	$2.99	☐
HP#11647	GIVE A MAN A BAD NAME by Roberta Leigh	$2.99	☐
HR#03293	THE MAN WHO CAME FOR CHRISTMAS by Bethany Campbell	$2.89	☐
HR#03308	RELATIVE VALUES by Jessica Steele	$2.89	☐
SR#70589	CANDY KISSES by Muriel Jensen	$3.50	☐
SR#70598	WEDDING INVITATION by Marisa Carroll	$3.50 U.S. $3.99 CAN.	☐
HI#22230	CACHE POOR by Margaret St. George	$2.99	☐
HAR#16515	NO ROOM AT THE INN by Linda Randall Wisdom	$3.50	☐
HAR#16520	THE ADVENTURESS by M.J. Rodgers	$3.50	☐
HS#28795	PIECES OF SKY by Marianne Willman	$3.99	☐
HS#28824	A WARRIOR'S WAY by Margaret Moore	$3.99 U.S. $4.50 CAN.	☐

(limited quantities available on certain titles)

	AMOUNT	$
DEDUCT:	**10% DISCOUNT FOR 2+ BOOKS**	$
ADD:	**POSTAGE & HANDLING**	$
	($1.00 for one book, 50¢ for each additional)	
	APPLICABLE TAXES*	$_____
	<u>**TOTAL PAYABLE**</u>	$_____
	(check or money order—please do not send cash)	

To order, complete this form and send it, along with a check or money order for the total above, payable to Harlequin Books, to: **In the U.S.:** 3010 Walden Avenue, P.O. Box 9047, Buffalo, NY 14269-9047; **In Canada:** P.O. Box 613, Fort Erie, Ontario, L2A 5X3.

Name: _____

Address: _____ City: _____

State/Prov.: _____ Zip/Postal Code: _____

*New York residents remit applicable sales taxes.
  Canadian residents remit applicable GST and provincial taxes.

HBACK-JM2